George McK. Steele

Rudimentary Ethics

George McK. Steele

Rudimentary Ethics

ISBN/EAN: 9783337390440

Printed in Europe, USA, Canada, Australia, Japan

Cover: Foto ©Andreas Hilbeck / pixelio.de

More available books at **www.hansebooks.com**

RUDIMENTARY ETHICS.

A Text-Book for High Schools and Academies.

GEO. M. STEELE, D.D., LL.D.,

PRINCIPAL OF WESLEYAN ACADEMY,

AND AUTHOR OF "RUDIMENTARY PSYCHOLOGY," "RUDIMENTARY ECONOMICS,"
AND "OUTLINES OF BIBLE STUDY."

PREFACE.

THIS volume, like a similar previous one on Psychology, is intended to meet a want in our academies and high schools. It professes no new discoveries in the ethical field, and no especially novel method of instruction. The design is to set forth the more essential principles of ethics in clear, simple, and familiar language, in their logical connections and with adherence to scientific forms.

The book is not a compilation; though doubtless very many of the thoughts presented may have been given by other writers, and have been absorbed by the author during years of reading in connection with instruction to successive classes of pupils.

On a few topics the writer has ventured to present views differing from those taught by the great majority of ethical philosophers. This is particularly true in respect to the doctrine of *Conscience*. It has seemed to him that the theories on this subject held by many of even our ablest writers have been confused and indefinite. Still, the fault, if fault there be, is doubtless one of phraseology rather than of essential principle. It is evidently better and simpler where we have several faculties, each with its separate function, to keep these separate under separate names, than to group them all together under a single name, which after all indicates no special function. Conscience and Judgment have been confused; and " moral faculty," and " moral sense," and " moral impulse," are much used, but not accurately defined. If Judgment is precisely the same faculty when exercised upon moral subjects that it is when exercised upon any other subject, and if Conscience, as is universally admitted, whatever else it does, always impels us to do what we judge to be right, why extend it to another function which already has a name of its own?

Similar but less pronounced variations from general standards will be found in respect to a few other topics.

Theoretical ethics has been treated with much brevity, as it was the intention to devote the work almost exclusively to practical morals.

G. M. S.

Wilbraham, Mass.

CONTENTS.

v

BOOK I.

THEORETICAL OUTLINE.

RUDIMENTARY ETHICS.

CHAPTER I.

FREEDOM OF HUMAN ACTION.

Ethics is the science of moral conduct. It is usually divided into Theoretical and Practical Ethics. Strictly speaking, the former is the science as presenting in systematic form the principles on which right moral action rests. The latter is the application of these principles to human conduct, and consists mainly of rules for the regulation of this conduct. Though a brief survey of the underlying principles seems essential to a clear understanding of the subject, this volume will be devoted chiefly to Practical Ethics.

There are certain terms in constant use in our language, and corresponding terms in other languages, to which one attaches definite meanings; such as *innocence* and *guilt, condemnation, approval* and *disapproval, responsibility, good* and *evil conduct.* But these terms really mean nothing unless our actions are free; that is, determined by ourselves and uncaused by any extraneous power. The very definition of an action would imply this. This definition is as follows: —

An act or action in the strict sense of the words, is *the intentional putting forth of an effort by an intelligent being,*

Terms implying free agency.

1

or one capable of setting before him an object or end, and the means of achieving it. This implies a personality, that is, a Will, and freedom in its exercise. This putting forth is by the power of the Will, and is known as **Volition**. But it involves more than this; namely, the selection of the object to be accomplished in preference to any other. This is the power of **Choice,** and implies a purpose or **intention**.

What is an act?

The fact that there are certain philosophers now, as there have been in the past, who insist upon the theory that man is not free, that all his actions are controlled by forces that he cannot resist, and that his character is thus determined, not by influences to which he exposes himself, but by influences to which without any choice of his own he is exposed, render it necessary that we should discuss to some extent that constituent of man's nature denominated the **Will**.

SECTION 1. — THE WILL.

The phenomena of the soul are of three kinds, and are usually set forth under a threefold division, as the **Intellect,** the **Sensibilities,** and the **Will**. This is not a separation of the soul into **parts,** since it is one and indivisible; but a classification of its energies and susceptibilities. The Intellect is the mind perceiving, judging, reasoning, knowing, etc. The Sensibilities are the mind feeling, that is, enjoying, suffering, craving, and impelling. The Will is the mind choosing, determining, putting forth effort. It is the executive power of the soul.

Threefold character of the Soul.

The relation of these faculties to one another is that of **the conditioning and the conditioned.** The Intellect is the first and lowest, as being a condition for the others. There can be no feeling except in view of some revealed fact, that is, of something known. I am glad or sorry, if at all, because of something which is made known to me ; and it is impossible to conceive of an emotion which is not occasioned by some knowledge or belief. So, too, the Will acts only when some desire or emotion is present in the soul. There must be some impulse, or motive, some reason for its acting.

Relation of conditioning and conditioned.

There are two functions of the Will; namely, Choice and Volition. There are always two or more acts or courses of action before the mind when the Will is called into exercise, and it must determine between them. In other words, there must be **Choice**. It is to be noted that the mind *must* choose. Whatever we may conclude concerning the question of freedom as the result of this discussion, it is not free to decline to choose. There is a necessity in this case. Having chosen which of several acts it will perform, **Volition** naturally follows. This is *the effort of the will to carry its choice into effect*. In many cases, perhaps in most, it follows instantly on the choice, but not always. I may make a choice to perform a certain act to-morrow; but the volition will not ensue until that time comes. It is even possible that in the interim something may occur to change my purpose, and so the volition may never follow. But when I determine to perform an act at once, the volition necessarily follows. Dr. Hopkins teaches that the freedom of the Will belongs to the power of Choice and not to that of Volition. This seems to me somewhat doubtful, though the fact that the Volition in certain cases necessarily follows the act of Choice is perhaps in favor of this view.

Two functions of the Will.

The Volition not always immediate upon the action of Choice.

Volition is not the physical effort, but an effort of the mind to perform an act. I may decide to leave the room,

Volition an effort of the mind.

and forthwith proceed to put my purpose into execution; but I find that the door is locked. Nevertheless, there has been a complete act of the Will, a Choice, and a Volition. In this case there has been also a physical effort. But I may stop short of that. Before I get to the door I may find that it is locked. So I put forth no further physical effort. It is even possible that before I put forth the physical effort, I may find that I am paralyzed, and though I essay to move, I cannot make the physical effort. The action of the Will is, however, still complete, the Choice and the Volition have both been made.

SECTION 2. — ARGUMENTS IN FAVOR OF FREEDOM.

The following are the chief reasons for believing in human freedom.

1. Our Consciousness testifies to it. Every man is conscious, when two objects or acts are presented to him, that

Testimony of Consciousness.

he may choose either. When there must be a choice between them, or when there is such an alternative that one must be taken and the other refused, he always recognizes it as a fact that he is not compelled to take either, though he must take one.

Nor can it be avoided by saying he may choose neither, for this is a case when to refuse one is virtually to choose the other; and if there be a case where both may be refused, still there is a choice. For instance, he may change his position or retain it. He may prefer to choose neither, but that is to choose to remain as he is. In any case he is certain that whichever he decides to do, he might have decided to do the other. It is true that a man is some-times deceived, and that of what he believes himself to be conscious he is not conscious; yet these instances are so manifestly infrequent and exceptional that they do not materially affect the question.

The simple fact is, that if we cannot trust our conscious-ness we cannot trust anything, and thus nothing will be certain to us. This should settle the matter. Further-more, if there were any force in the argument that men are in exceptional instances deceived as to the testimony of their consciousness, it still ought not to shake convic-tion concerning a matter in which nearly the whole race in all ages and under the widest possible diversity of conditions agree.

2. **The way human conduct is universally regarded** confirms the conviction just spoken of. Men regard themselves as having done what they were under no necessity Universal of doing, and reproach themselves for their Conviction. folly or their wickedness. Even men who deny this free-dom talk and act as though they regarded it as a fact. They reproach their fellows for actions as being base and unworthy and vicious, and approve and praise what is noble and heroic or virtuous.

3. The **Language** of all nations, ancient and modern, civilized and barbarous, and even savage, unmistakably indicates this. The remarkably significant word Testimony of **ought,** which has its equivalent in so many lan- Language. guages, is a simple instance of this kind. Obviously what ought to be done can be done, and we have no right to say that a man ought to do what some extraneous power prevents him from doing. The terms *guilt, respon-sibility, punishment, repentance, remorse, condemnation,*

and so many others in all tongues, that if obliterated from
the vocabulary of any nation would seriously demoralize
the language, show this. Men are not responsible for
doing what they are compelled to do, nor for failing to do
what is impossible.

4. It is further implied in the existence of **laws and rules
of action.** The moral law, as believed to be imposed by
Law assumes the Ruler of the universe, would be, were there
the Freedom no free agency of the individual, not only like
of Individual
Action. the natural law in the absolute certainty of its
execution, but at the same time misleading and preposterous in that, unlike it, it is accompanied by penalties for its
violation and assumes the possibility of disobedience to
its mandates. The laws of nations and of families go on
the same supposition. It would be senseless for a legislature to enact laws, or for a monarch to issue edicts, if it
were the fact that some extraneous force determines obedience and disobedience to them. So of the government of
families and other cognate societies, in which, if the members have no power of choice, the authority of those who
govern can have no effect on conduct.

5. **Promises and Contracts** imply a belief in freedom of
action. The promiser has not the slightest doubt that he
will be free to attempt what he promises, and the promisee
accepts and relies upon such promise in the same natural
conviction. It is considered a valid reason for the non-
performance of a contract if there are unforeseen obstacles
which render the performance impossible.

SECTION 3. — ARGUMENTS AGAINST FREEDOM.

The arguments against human freedom are curious and
interesting, and might be convincing to many but for the
overwhelming force of those for the affirmative.

1. There is the supposed power of the strongest motive. It is admitted that the mind acts in view of motives, and that it frequently yields to that which it re- **The Power of** gards as the most desirable on the whole. Is it **Motives.** not natural to believe that it is the strongest in such cases that prevails? But what is meant by the "strongest" motive? To this question there is no satisfactory reply. The only definite answer that can be made, as it would seem, is that it is the motive which prevails, and so we get an argument in a circle.

The doctrine of the power of motives is altogether mechanical, and inapplicable to spiritual action. If we are to regard the motives as forces compelling the action of the mind, it is pretty likely to be the case that in the conflict of two such forces impelling the mind in different directions it would move in neither direction, but in a line between the two after the analogy of the composition of forces. For instance, if I stand at one angle of a parallelogram and am attracted by some object in front of me, and at the same time by another object off at my right hand, according to this theory I should go to neither of them, but to a point somewhere between them.

It is clearly possible for motives to influence the mind and at the same time to have no compelling power. We are to make the distinction here as elsewhere **Difference be-** between cause and condition. The former **tween Cause** compels an effect; the latter is the reason why **tion.** the effect takes place. Motive is a condition and not a cause of action.

2. It is urged in favor of necessity that if we know the character of the man we can generally foretell what his conduct will be under certain circumstances. It

is true that we can frequently anticipate what a person with whom we are intimately acquainted, or whose principles

Human Pre-science of Human Conduct. and manner of life we know by report, would be likely to do in a given exigency. For instance, we have great confidence that a friend whom we know as a stanch total abstainer, if at a party where wine should be on the table, would turn down his glasses. I have lived many years by a gentleman of strict integrity in all his conduct. When word is brought to me that he has deliberately lied about a certain matter of personal interest, I do not for a moment believe the report, and I think it much more likely that the reporter lies than that my neighbor does. But these cases, and hundreds of others like them, are cases of very great likelihood, not of certainty. Character is not so fixed as to be unchangeable. Great revolutions sometimes take place; and so many are the exceptions, that the French proverb says, "It is the unexpected that happens." It may be said that if we perfectly knew a person's character we could perfectly predict his conduct under perfectly given conditions. But this is begging the question. It is impossible that we should know all this, and it is preposterous to assert what would be the effect of an impossibility. Furthermore, it is more than doubtful that if the conditions were granted it would disprove freedom. For, as we shall see directly, a man might be in a condition that he would certainly do certain things and not do others, and still be under no compulsion whatever.

3. It is further said that the power of habit is such that

Power of Habit. it becomes at last irresistible. If this were so, it would not prove that a habit *must* become irresistible, as it may be controlled and checked in its be-

ginnings if not later. It is no doubt true that a man may
so yield himself to bad motives that the good motives
may be displaced and that there will be no motive to
a good deed. But this does not imply inability to do
otherwise than he does, but a stubborn disinclination. So
a good man may suppress and extirpate all motives to
wrong action, and will then not sin, not because he cannot, but because he does not want to, just as he does not
leap off the top of a house, not because he cannot, but
because there is ordinarily no motive for him to do so.

4. Another assigned reason for denying the freedom of
the individual is found in the Divine prescience. If God
is omniscient, he must know beforehand all our Divine Fore-
acts. If he knows that a certain act will take knowledge.
place, then it must take place, and thus all human conduct
is previously fixed. So runs the argument. To avoid
this conclusion, some believers in freedom have been led
to deny God's foreknowledge.

There are two fallacies in this reasoning which are not
far to seek. The first is in the assumption that God must
foreknow as men foreknow; that is, after a Difference be-
scientific fashion. Men foretell eclipses, the tween Human
and Divine
rising and setting of certain heavenly bodies, Foreknowl-
the ebb and flow of the tides, the coming and edge.
going of the seasons, because they know the causes that
produce and the laws that govern these events. Hence it
is assumed that God knows in the same way. But this
assumption is entirely gratuitous. It is at least conceivable that the Infinite Intelligence has other means of knowing than those which belong to finite men. He may know
events and actions beforehand, not because he knows the
laws and causes implied in them, but directly and in them-

selves. Even men have intuitive knowledge of certain facts, and it is easy to believe that God has infinitely greater powers of cognition.

But in the second place, the theory assumes that to know an event *will* take place, is the same as knowing _{That an Event} that it *must* take place. To know the latter is _{will occur,
not the same} to know the former, but to know the former _{as that it} does not imply the latter. Looking forward is, _{must occur.} in this respect, no way different from looking backward. Because I know that an event has taken place, is evidently not the same as to know it must have taken place. God looks forward and foreknows the acts of men, but he so far knows them to be unnecessary that he declares his purpose to punish the perpetration of some of them, and to reward the doers of others of them.

SECTION 4. — HABIT IN RELATION TO THE WILL.

In the previous section, Habit was spoken of as relating to the indications of a man's future conduct. The sub-
Habit defined. ject, perhaps, demands some amplification. By Habit is meant the increased facility in the performance of certain acts, which comes from frequent repetition. It is not peculiar to mental conduct, but is characteristic as well of the physical acts. The little child takes its first steps with very great difficulty, and at some peril. Its first attempts to balance itself on its legs are apt to result in a tumble; but continued and reiterated effort overcomes the difficulty, and soon enables it to stand firmly, to walk confidently, and even to run, and perform the most surprising feats, without the least danger. It is so with all the members of the body. It is not the less so with the mind. Certain mental operations

at first appear impossible; but persistence soon creates not only their possibility, but ease and skill in their performance. To most minds efforts in memorizing, in trying to comprehend certain thoughts, in literary composition, in any form of conveying our thoughts to others, prove a very difficult task. To become a scholar requires constant action and perpetual repetition, till at last it becomes to some, at least, almost a second nature, and study is performed with both ease and enjoyment.

This law of habit extends itself to the moral conduct, and is of very great importance there. Our wills, to some extent, come under the influence of this law. The first profane oath of the boy startles himself, and brings with it self-reproach and condemnation. The second time it is easier; and within no very long time he repeats it without compunction, and possibly comes at last to swear as he breathes. He finds it hard to resist the tendency, even if he would. So the appetites and passions indulged beyond their natural limit grow into habits that tyrannize over their subject till it seems impossible to break away from them.

The Will affected by this Law.

The virtues as well as the vices are subject to the same law. At first it is with an effort involving sacrifice perhaps, and self-denials, that we take up certain duties and abandon certain immoralities. Little by little we come to feel the restraint and constraint less and less, and at last our action or our abstinence comes to be an easy and natural act. Not only particular virtues and vices are affected in this way, but the general purpose and plan of one's moral life is subject to this law. A man under the conviction that he is leading an unworthy life while following the dictates of

How it affects Virtues and Vices.

appetite, or passion, or self-love, resolves to be governed by his conscience, and to live uprightly and justly. He will find at first that his way is beset with difficulties. He meets with constantly recurring inducements to turn aside from the way which he has determined to follow. There are powerful tendencies to be resisted; and he must exert all his energies, and guard with scrutiny all his steps. But gradually the force of former habits is diminished, and he becomes habituated to his new course. The effort, the conscious sacrifice, is less and less, and the vigilance may almost cease. We know some such persons to whom it seems as if a wrong act would be impossible. Evil desires in such a mind, as good desires in an evil mind, have been suppressed and extirpated by disuse, and there is no longer any motive contrary to the general purpose to be overcome.

In view of these facts, the relation of Habit to the Will and Conscience is of very great importance. The habit of indulging an appetite, or cherishing any desire, or of any kind of wrong-doing, may become so strong that it seems practically irresistible. Doubtless it is not what it seems. The simple fact is, that while the individual

One may lose the Desire without losing the Ability.

has not lost the ability to do what he ought to do, he has lost all desire to do it; and since desire furnishes occasion or condition for any action, the absence of desire to act in a particular way renders it certain that he will not so act. But it is even doubtful that there is any case in which all desire for virtuous action is wanting. There are multitudes of instances in which the power of evil habit has become so great that it seems impossible to break it; and yet by some intense effort, with great pain and much sacrifice, the soul has wrenched itself away from its thraldom, and achieved its emancipation. That there are thousands of other instances in which the ability exists, yet the lower impulse is allowed to govern, may be reasonably inferred.

But even if we suppose it possible that Habit ever does become so despotic that the will is paralyzed, and the individual is no longer a free agent, this would be only a penal consequence of the crime he has committed against himself, when, in the unconditioned exercise of his will, he deliberately chose a course which was likely to lead to this debasement. *We are responsible for our Evil Choices, and therefore for their Effects.* It makes nothing against the entire freedom of the individual: he freely chose his own course of life and all that might be involved in it.

We have an equally good and more pleasing illustration in the case of a man who elects to do that which is right, and forms a virtuous habit of life. We are not to presume that he will ever arrive at a point where he *cannot* do wrong; but he will *Habit as related to Virtue.* doubtless arrive at a position by gradual development where he *will have no desire* to do anything which he perceives to be wrong, and for that reason will never do so. We must remember that men will never do what they have no motive for doing, however clear the ability may be to do it; and motive implies some kind of desire. We have innumerable partial illustrations in actual life of what is meant here. As a rule we do not make a practice of putting our hands into the fire, and this not because we cannot do so. There are extreme exceptional instances where this has been done, as in the case of Archbishop Cranmer, and the Roman soldier Mucius Scævola representing his people in the presence of a hostile king, and illustrating the fortitude of his fellow-soldiers. We do not ordinarily do it, because we don't want to: there is no motive for doing it. So of a hundred other things which we do or refrain from doing: not because the contrary is impossible, but from the absence of any degree or kind of desire.

I have spoken of these as partial illustrations. They are not complete for the reason that there are exceptional cases where a motive does exist to do the unusual thing, and where, for the sake of some greater good, the disagreeable thing will be done, as when the life of a child or of a friend is in peril.

We have some of us been accustomed to think of the glorified saints and angels as beyond the possibility of sinning. That a state is conceivable in which they will never sin, I have no manner of doubt; but this is not because of inability, but because there will be no desire of anything involving moral evil: there is an infinite aversion to wrong-doing, and therefore no motive furnishing an occasion for it.

It is also clearly conceivable that, under the power of persistent and cultivated evil habit, souls may reach a stage in which there is not the slightest desire for virtuous action or pious conduct. Their case may be hopeless, not because of an inability to practise righteousness, but because there is an infinite aversion to it, and consequently no motive furnishing a condition for such action.

Such seems to me to be the relation of Habit to the Will. It may become a gigantic motive influencing but not compelling the Will, suppressing and annihilating all counter-motives, and thus destroying all conditions precedent for particular actions, or courses of action. The Will cannot choose an object which does not present itself in the consciousness. But in all cases where more than one such object is presented, it may elect freely; and there is no power, finite or even infinite, which will coerce its choice.

CHAPTER II.

THE BASIS OF ETHICS.

SECTION 1. — ORIGIN OF THE CONCEPTION OF THE MORAL QUALITY IN ACTIONS.

ALL sciences start with certain observed phenomena, and are developed and brought to perfection by classifying these phenomena, ascertaining their mutual relations, the order of change or progress to which they are subject, and the various laws that govern them. In the physical sciences the phenomena appeal to the senses. There are also metaphysical ideas, first principles and intuitive truths of which, when occasion is furnished, we become cognizant by the very constitution of the mind. The phenomena of the mind are as apprehensible by us through what is popularly called Consciousness, or the Inner-Sense, as are the phenomena of the external world through Sense-perception. Through the Pure Reason we have space, time, number, personal identity, etc. We know that a part of a thing is less than the whole, not that two quantities, each of which is equal to a third quality, are equal to each other, and that the same cause under the same conditions will always produce the same effect.

All science begins with observation.

In all nations, and in all generations of men, a distinction has been made between **Right** and **Wrong**, and a belief has prevailed that there is not only a difference between these two conceptions, but an irreconcilable antagonism between them. Just as men made a distinc- Universality tion between beauty and deformity, wisdom of the moral and folly, intelligence and ignorance, so they conception. make the distinction between Right and Wrong. The standard is not always the same in the last of these cases any more than in the others. What in some communities are regarded as right, are in others regarded as wrong, and *vice versa.* But everywhere and always there is some standard of moral conduct, and a moral quality in human actions is recognized.

Do all actions have a moral quality?

It is important to ascertain the precise place of the moral quality in relation to an action. In the perform- ance of an act, there are four parts of the pro- Location of cess. First, there is the **conception** of the object the moral quality of an to be accomplished; secondly, there is the **choice** action. between doing and not doing, or the resolution to do or not do; thirdly, the **volition** or effort put forth; and fourthly, the **intention.** Now, the moral quality is not found in either of the first three, since these might be precisely the same, whether the action were good or bad; but in the **intention,** inasmuch as the same act would be wholly bad if performed with one intention, and wholly good if per- formed with another. A man who shoots another and kills him, if he does it in malice, is regarded as deeply criminal; whereas, if he does it in self-defence, or to pre- serve the lives of his children threatened by a robber, he is held innocent.

Whether all actions have a moral quality, then, depends upon the answer to the question whether the action has a moral end in view. If I go to a bookstore and am in a state of doubt whether to buy a volume of essays by a distinguished author, or an historical work of equal celebrity, it would seem almost obvious that no moral character could possibly attach to my action, that it would be decided on entirely prudential grounds, and would not be wrong to do either. So if I sit down to a dinner where two dishes are set before me, there would seem to be no ethical character in my choice; it would be purely a matter of taste.

Do all actions have a moral quality?

Yet even in such instances a moral quality might be present in the act. In that of the books, the fact that one is evidently more profitable than the other, would make it my duty to take that. In the matter of the two dishes, it might easily be the fact that one would be more nourishing or be followed by less unfavorable consequences than the other, and it would clearly be my duty to give the preference to that one. It is no doubt conceivable that two acts may present themselves so exactly alike in their moral effect that the choice between them would have no ethical character. These are exceptional instances; but in a considerable number of cases the consequences as good or bad cannot be foreseen, or would not be thought of by the actor, and would therefore have no moral character. Still, there is little doubt that a much larger proportion of our acts are subject to moral conditions than we are accustomed to estimate.

SECTION 2. — THEORIES OF THE BASIS OF OBLIGATION.

We have seen that the conception of a moral quality in conduct exists universally among men. Whence, then, does it arise? Where do we find the ultimate authority and indisputable ethical standard? There are several theories on this subject.

The first that we shall consider is the **Utilitarian Theory.** According to this, the motive of right and wrong is derived from that of **the greatest good.** Very early in the history of the race, men would learn to estimate what would be for their greatest happiness, and in process of time this came to be regarded as an obligation; that is, a compliance with it was looked upon as **right,** and a violation of it as **wrong.** There are two principal forms of this theory; namely, one in which the moral idea is supposed to be evolved from the individual regard for personal welfare; the other, where it is derived from that of the highest good of the whole, or at least of the greater number. Probably these two forms are reconcilable, and very likely the latter is derived from the former. It is not unlikely that the highest welfare of the individual, if regarded broadly enough, would coincide with the highest welfare of the community or the race. But few individuals would be able to take that view of the subject without a considerable process of education. *Utilitarianism.* *Two forms.*

The main objections to this theory lie in the facts, first, that the two ideas, the ethical and that of the greatest good, are totally unlike; second, that there are numerous acts in which the thought of the greatest happiness is in many instances obviously altogether absent from the mind of the actor. Upon the former of these it is unnecessary to dilate. As to the latter, let us take a single case. The mother, finding her child in peril, rushes to its rescue without a thought of whether her action, which may not only involve some *Objections to this theory.*

inconvenience, but perhaps some suffering to herself, will add to her own happiness or the happiness of the community. It is true, also, that she does not consider the demand of duty; still, it is what would be duty, were no other impulses present. It may be said that this is the prompting of maternal love. But it may easily be shown, as we shall see in the progress of this study, that love is the perfection of the moral law, and that it so involves all duties and obligations that they cease to be felt in the form of restraint or constraint, being changed to inclinations and appetences. So far is self-interest, or a desire for one's own welfare, from being an essential element in moral action, there is a very large range of conduct in which it does not at all appear.

Another reason for rejecting the utilitarian theory is that the ideas of the right and of the useful are entirely distinct in our minds. Still another is that in a vast number of cases we should find it impossible to determine what would be the highest good, either of the individual or of society. Again, in the Providential administration of human affairs, deeds which are in themselves of the worst character are very likely to be so overruled that unmeasured good comes from them.

Our conception of the two ideas distinct.

A second theory of the origin of the ethical idea is that of Authority. The child in the family is taught that there must be obedience to the parents, and he soon comes to have a feeling of obligation, or sense of duty. This is further cultivated by the relations of civil society and subjection to government. It becomes still more sacred in the relations of a religious society and the government of the church. In close connection with

Theory of Authority.

this last, or possibly without it, emerges the thought of Divine government, and the supreme authority of the Infinite Creator and Ruler of the Universe, and the conviction that this authority is asserted in the Sacred Scriptures as containing a revelation of His will concerning human conduct.

No doubt these are all influential in the cultivation of moral character; but that is not sufficient to account for the *origin* of the sentiment of universal obligation. This must first exist in the human mind before there can be any tendency to recognize authority of any sort. Even the highest authority — that of the Divine Ruler — would appeal in vain to the individual soul, were the latter not so constituted that the feeling of obligation would rise spontaneously on its proper occasion.

This brings us to the third theory, namely, the Intuitional. The phenomena which lie at the basis of the science of ethics are included in and imply Intuition-psychical phenomena. They are apprehended alism. from the very constitution of the mind as soon as the occasion for them presents itself. As soon as certain acts are brought before the mind, either in fact or in conception, the moral quality of them is discerned, just as men, when they perceive a body, know that it occupies space, or as they know, when they see an apple cut into quarters, that a quarter is less than the whole. According to this theory, the ethical idea is original, a first principle evolved or derived from no other idea previously in the mind.

In rejecting the first two theories, it is not intended to be denied that there are certain important facts connected with them which are essential and useful as subsidiary

to the application of the third theory, and in determining
the establishment of a right code of conduct. Though we
The first two may not accept the doctrine that the concep-
theories to tion of a moral quality is evolved from that of
be rejected,
but not with- the greatest happiness, either of the individual
out value. or of society, it is unquestionably true that the
observance of the moral law, or the rule of right conduct,
always ultimately coincides with, and is conducive to,
this great happiness. It is in this way that men, without
a revelation or other positive instruction, learn what kind
of conduct is virtuous and what is vicious. Those who
believe in the Divine government must believe also that
God has so constituted the world and its intelligent inhabitants, that, when the conduct of the latter is right, a
part of the result at least will be their greatest happiness.
Hence the observance of the moral law will always tend
to the well-being of the subject of it.

It is also no doubt true that obedience to parents, and
submission to civil government and to the precepts of
Scriptures as expressing the Divine will, prepare the mind
for the appreciation and acceptance of moral law. It is
not necessary to discuss the question whether God's will
is the sole foundation and basis of the moral law, or
whether, as some eminent thinkers maintain, this basis is
in *the very nature of things*, and that even the Divine character is to be judged by its conformity to it; for in either
case it is obvious that God's character, and consequently
his law and government, are thus conformed to the eternal
law of right; and therefore whatever expression he has
given of his will must coincide with this. So that we
need seek no further than to know what is the Divine will
in order to know what is the ultimate authority. Those,

therefore, who accept the Bible as a Divine revelation will be justified in making it their supreme moral standard. But underneath all this, and essential to it, there is strong reason for believing that the idea of a moral quality in actions is intuitively discerned, and that it is a product of the constitution that has been given us, and therefore universal and necessary.

CHAPTER III.

SPRINGS OF ACTION.

WE are excited to action by certain impulses and incentives which are a part of our constitution. These may be
Divisions of divided into five groups; namely, the **Appetites**,
the subject. the **Desires**, the **Affections**, **Self-love**, and **Conscience**.
We will consider them in order.

SECTION 1. — THE APPETITES.

The **Appetites** are cravings for such things as are for the well-being of the body and continuance of the race.
Definition. They are **hunger, thirst, sex,** and perhaps the **cravings for air and sleep.** They are for the most part, and primarily, periodical and self-limited. In a healthy and well-balanced person the appetites are satisfied when they have been indulged so far as is good for the body. But they are liable to be abused in such ways as to minister to physical disorder, and the degradation of the soul. Such craving is prompted, not by any proper demand of the appetites themselves, but by certain concomitants which constitute a fictitious want clamoring in various degrees for indulgence. For instance, when one eats of a certain kind of food there is, besides the satisfaction of the normal appetite, the pleasure of the palate and other organs; and there is frequently an inducement to

prolong this enjoyment by continued eating, and this is usually to the detriment of the body.

This is more especially the case in the indulgence of **artificial appetites.** There are certain articles for which no person, except those hereditarily affected, has an appetite. Tobacco is a conspicuous instance. Probably Artificial no human being ever naturally enjoyed the use Appetites. of this drug. The first experiment with it almost always results in nausea. Yet to multitudes it not only becomes a luxury, but the occasion of a slavish habit, which even when it is felt to be a physical evil of very great magnitude, they have not the energy to shake off. The same is true of other narcotics. It is terribly true in respect to alcoholic beverages, the use of which has become a vice of incalculable magnitude, destroying multitudes of lives, ruining character, and bringing poverty, degradation, and untold suffering, to thousands of families.

I have spoken of the **appetites** as among the incentives to human effort. In their normal action the satisfaction of them is a source of pleasure. But for this Normal use of we should be liable to neglect much that is the Appetites. essential to our well-being. But for hunger, and the pleasure of its satisfaction, we might be indisposed to eat at proper times, or in proper quantities, or of the most nourishing food. The craving for food also spurs men up to the effort to secure it, and thus we have productive labor. Men do not naturally like to work,—it is only the pressure of some want; and but for this many, perhaps most, would not work. But in these, as in other springs of action, there needs to be some check and balance among the several incentives which will keep them all within their designed limits.

SECTION 2. — THE DESIRES.

These are cravings of the mind for such things as are for the well-being of the soul. We will consider briefly the chief of them.

Definition.

There is first the desire for **Continued Existence**. We are constituted with a love of life. We instinctively shrink from death, not merely because of its possible agonies, nor its sequences, but because it implies the cessation of our present conscious condition. It is only when men have, either by their own misuse of the blessings of life wrought themselves into a position where the provisions for their happiness have become utterly unavailable, or when, by assiduous religious and spiritual culture, they have come to have an earnest faith in the superior blessedness of the future world, that they ever welcome death, — in the former case because they are disgusted with life, and have no faith in the future ; in the latter, because, having made the best of their life, they accept the glorious promise of that which is to come. Both these classes are doubtless exceptional. The great mass of men love life ; the desire is made useful by inciting them to care for their health, to guard against accidents, and to instinctively seek to protect themselves in sudden danger.

Utility of this Desire.

Another of the desires is that for **Wealth**. If life is to continue, there must be means of supporting it ; and these means are, in part at least, what constitute wealth. This may exist in a very small, an almost imperceptible, degree ; the meanest shelter, the coarsest and poorest raiment, the earnings of a single day, the provisions which a few meals, and scanty at that, may exhaust, are still of the nature of wealth. It is a legitimate desire to secure so much of this as will make one comfortable, and as Liabilities to will be a defence against want, both in the pres- Perversion. ent and for the future. This desire, like the appetites and other cravings, may become inordinate, and eventuate in the vices of avarice and covetousness, and lead to extortion and fraud, and may result in robbery and cognate crimes. Still, in itself, and within its legitimate limits, it is of great utility, tending to promote industry, temperance, frugality, thoughtfulness, carefulness, and other virtues.

The desire for **Knowledge** is also to be considered. The means of preserving life, and all that makes life valuable, depends upon the knowledge we have. But it is not merely for the sake of ulterior ends that we are incited to seek knowledge : we desire it for its own sake. There is, in earliest childhood, a restless curiosity, an eagerness to get at the secrets of things, which leads even A Natural the infant to dissect its own toys to satisfy this Desire early craving. In more mature minds it prompts to Manifested. great sacrifices, to protracted and laborious study, to years of minute investigation. It is out of these labors and sacrifices that sciences are born and philosophies are constructed, that marvellous discoveries are made, and that the most wonderful inventions are rendered possible by which labor is saved and production is increased a hundred and a thousand fold. This also may be abused, though it is less likely to be than some other desires. But in the eagerness of the pursuit of knowledge, health is sometimes sacrificed, and life shortened, or cut off in its prime.

The desire of **Power.** This, too, is a proper and inno-
Not only Desirable, but Obligatory. cent desire. It is subsidiary to some of the others; yet power is often sought for its own sake, and its possession gives satisfaction to the possessor. It is, no doubt, not only legitimate for every good man to be as powerful as possible, but it is obligatory upon him. Such a man being devoted to the production of all kinds of moral utilities, both for himself and for the community, and as well for the whole race, must needs make himself as influential as his condition permits. Capable of Perversion. A bad man will seek power for bad ends; and, like all else that he does, he may in this be actuated by pernicious motives. But this desire, like that for possession, is easily carried to excess, however virtuous its beginnings may be. Hence it prompts to various vices. The selfish ambition of man has been the cause of a large part of the evils which prevail in humanity, and of the degradation and suffering of large masses in our communities.

The desire for the **Approbation of our fellow-men** is another of the inducements to action which affect all men. It is in our constitution, therefore universal. The reason for its existence is not far to seek. A man's usefulness and value as a member of human society would be almost or quite wholly wanting, were the good opinion of his fellow-members withheld from him. He could do little good to them, and get little good from them, if they should regard him with indifference or distrust. Like other desires, it may become a vice when indulged beyond its province. An inordinate desire for approbation becomes vanity, a foolish disposition, and one to be deprecated, and, in certain of its forms, to be despised.

The desire of **Liberty**. This differs so much from the other desires that some eminent writers refuse to reckon it among them. Instead of having special objects of its own, it has reference to all the other desires; and the craving which charac-terizes it is a craving for the privilege of gratifying them. We can scarcely conceive of its existence, were there no other desires, and were these not in some way restricted. It is the removal of restriction for which this craving makes demand; and so far forth it would seem to be per-fectly subsidiary, though perhaps not subordinate. Still, it so far partakes of the nature of desire as to be a pow-erful incentive to action. A large proportion of the efforts put forth by individuals and societies is for the removal of the restraint which is put upon their actions, and which hinders their enjoyment. It is a proper and legitimate de-sire when urging to the breaking down of the barriers which prevent the free action of the soul, or the removing of obstacles to the growth and development or to the action, of society; but it easily degenerates into the vice of license, as, sometimes, when it leads to the disregard of wholesome rules of conduct, or allows the passions and appetites to have free scope, and overwhelm and debauch the soul; or, in other words, when it would give the lower powers of the soul control over those that are higher and nobler.

Differs from the other Desires.

Liberty not License.

The desire of **Society**, like that of **Liberty**, is by some writers refused a place in this list. But like Liberty it so far partakes of the nature of desire that for our present purpose it may properly be considered here. Man was constituted for society. No human individual is sufficient unto himself. Every man

Society es-sential to man's com-pleteness.

has something that others, possibly all others, lack. No one, without the aid of others, can secure more than a small part of what is essential to his well-being. Every man is not only a small fraction of humanity, but he is also a small fraction of his really complete self, if dependent solely on his own **Individuality.** Hence each man is essential to every other of, at least, a large group. Association is thus indispensable. Men must form societies for economic as well as for political pur-

Association and Individuality.

poses and for all the great ends which they propose to themselves. This association may not be sought in a way to destroy individuality. On the contrary, Individuality in its fullest development is essential to the highest type of Society. Men associate most when they differ most, and this *difference* is what constitutes their *individuality.* Two men who produce the same commodities are of very little use to each other economically. Two men who have precisely the same ideas would have no inducement to communicate with each other. Hence an organization of society on the basis of the suppression or diminution of individuality would be unprofitable and vicious. Man then being dependent on society, whatever he does to render society weak or inefficient reacts upon himself and is a damage to him. So also whenever society, by its agent the government, diminishes the individuality of its members by despotic measures or a tyrannical policy, it brings ultimate damage to itself.

SECTION 3. — THE AFFECTIONS.

The **Affections** are like the desires in the fact that they imply a craving for certain objects. They differ from

them in the fact that they are altruistic, or have refer- How they dif-
ence to others, while the desires are self-regard- How they dif-
ing. It is of the essence of love to seek to fer from the
promote the happiness of the object loved. The desires.
affections are usually divided into the **natural** and the
moral. The former are those which spring up spontaneously when the object of them presents itself. Natural and
The latter are those that may be cultivated. moral affec-
But, for the most part, all affections are pri- tions.
marily natural, and only take on a moral character when
they are liable to be prevented or suppressed by other
influences. Thus a child under the restraints of parental
discipline may be so devoted to some forbidden pleasure as
to regard its own gratification more than the affection
that ought to govern it; and this affection may diminish
or possibly cease. In all cases of this kind the condition
of the child is not only undutiful, but it is unnatural and
so far forth vicious. To resist and rectify this bad tendency becomes an obligation and so takes on a moral character. There are also cases in which there may spring up
spontaneously an affection towards an unworthy object, and
it may be a duty to check and neutralize it. Here also
the affection takes on a moral character.

The affections have also been by most writers divided
into **Benevolent** and **Malevolent**. These terms are objected
to by Dr. Hopkins as implying that the affections are
under the control of the will, as they are not wholly or
directly. The terms **Beneficent** and **Maleficent** have been
suggested as substitutes; but as the former have come to
be of nearly universal use, and are readily understood by
readers, it will be as well, so far as our present purpose is
concerned, to adhere to them.

The **Benevolent Affections** are *Love of kindred*, *Friendship*, *Love of country*, *Love of Humanity*, and *Sympathy*.

Different classes of Benevolent Affections. The Love of kindred embraces parental love, filial love, and fraternal love. They are natural and spontaneous affections, and spring up as soon as the objects of them are known. The strongest of these is parental love, and the love of the mother for her child has come to be the synonym of all great affection. These affections may become extravagant and inordinate. They may be perverted or interrupted or cease altogether. In this condition they indicate a moral character, and may thus be rectified only by moral means. The same is true in respect to the other affections according to their measure.

The **Malevolent Affections** are the opposite of the **Benevolent**; and as the latter are characterized by the desire to do Essential elements in the Malevolent Affections. the object of them some good, so Hatred, which is the essential element in Malevolent Affections, is characterized by a desire to do the object some harm. Foremost among the Malevolent Affections is **Anger,** and this is perhaps in some sense implied in all the rest; indeed, it is sometimes represented that the others are only modifications of this.

The question is sometimes raised whether Anger is Is Anger ever justifiable? ever justifiable. Unquestionably, when it takes the form of resentment of some evil deed, and the sentiment arises that such conduct is deserving of punishment, it is an innocent feeling. But when it passes beyond this, and implies hatred of the person, it cannot be justifiable. It is not unfrequently a wholly bad and forbidden passion, disagreeable to the subject and harmful to all affected by it.

Some of the modifications of Anger usually reckoned as separate malevolent affections, are **Indignation,** which indicates a more or less intense feeling of the culpability of an action accompanied by a sense of the ill-desert of the doer; **Wrath,** which is anger expressing itself in outward manifestations sometimes alarming to the objects of it; and **Fury,** a still more excited form of it in which the subject tends to lose all self-control. **Envy** and **Jealousy** are feelings that belong here. The former is a base feeling excited by beholding the success of another with whom we are in some way in competition, a hatred of him simply because he has succeeded better than ourselves. The latter is the state of mind into which one is thrown when a person to whom we are attached is suspected of bestowing his affection or friendship on another. More frequently than otherwise perhaps this feeling arises on mere suspicion when there is no ground for it. It is a painful, unreasonable sentiment, and is indicative of a mind weak and ill-balanced.

SECTION 4. — SELF-INTEREST.

This constituent of the affections also known as **Self-love,** and **Desire for one's own happiness,** is sometimes reckoned among the Desires; but it occupies so large a Why reckoned apart from the other desires. place among the incentives of human action, and is so powerful a force, that it seems altogether important that it be considered by itself. Another reason for this separate consideration is found in the fact that though partaking of the nature of the Desires, it radically differs from the other desires in this, that it can in no way be gratified except through the gratification of one or more of them. If a man can be supposed to exist in a condition in which all desires — and here we must take the word in its very broadest sense as including the appetites and the affections — are wanting, he might still have an eager craving for happiness which, nevertheless, it is impossible to satisfy either in whole or in part. Such is the condition called *hypochondria.* A person in this state may have the same ardent longing for happiness that others have, but he can think of nothing which will produce this happiness. In other words, while the desire for food, or for power, or for wealth, can be gratified directly, the desire for happiness can be gratified only through the medium of some other gratification.

But again Self-love differs from other desires in the characteristic that while the latter clamor for instant satisfaction, for the greatest immediate enjoyment, and have no reference to the future, Self-love takes account of this and seeks the largest amount of enjoyment on the whole. Hence there is frequently a struggle between this and some other inclination. We see it in infancy. The little child has its cake, a part of which it would like to keep till to-morrow; but it would also like to eat it now. Hence the common and suggestive proverb, "You cannot keep your cake and eat it too."

Self-love has reference to the future.

Illustration.

The young man who is earning money, but has only what he earns, may desire to save a part of his earnings and accumulate for the future. He may also desire to spend it on fine clothes, on entertainments, and high living. He cannot do both. Here is a man who has acquired a taste for alcoholic beverages. He has come to long for the excitement which they produce. He knows that if he indulges that appetite freely the consequences are likely to be his unfitness for any calling in life, and lack of respectability among men, and finally the ruin of both body and soul as well as the disgrace and misery of his family. He wants to be a competent and efficient workman, a respected and respectable member of society, to have property and a home, and to have his family in comfort and the enjoyment of the conveniences of life. He wants also the pleasure that comes from the indulgence of his appetite. He cannot have all these. There is a struggle. The prudent and sensible man suppresses the appetite, denies himself the present momentary gratification, and chooses the lasting good that lies in the future.

Primarily man does not like to labor, that is, to perform systematic and regular and protracted work. It is only as this is associated with the rewards of Natural labor, and the habit of years, that men come to aversion to love work. True, they then feel uneasy if labor. they are not accomplishing something. But originally it is mostly from the fear of want, and the desire of providing against it, and for the sake of larger enjoyments in the future, that they submit to this in the present. Toil and self-denial are the conditions of nearly all the enjoyments that men have in this world; and Self-love is the motive that impels to these.

We are to distinguish between Self-love and Selfishness, a distinction not always made. Self-love is a characteristic of our constitution, and is therefore not only legitimate, but of very great utility. A desire for one's own happiness, and seeking for one's own interest, can be justly condemned by no one. It has much to do, as has been shown, in limiting the appetites, desires, and affections, and compelling them to act within their own proper sphere. But Self-love has also its own limits; and it is when transgressing these limits that it becomes selfishness, which is a vicious and pernicious disposition. In other words, *Selfishness is inordinate Self-love.* When men pursue their own happiness in violation or disregard of the rights of others, or of any higher interest than their own enjoyment, then they become selfish. Selfishness is the author of most other sins, and to combat and suppress it is the chief moral obligation of every man. It presents itself in manifold forms; it is extremely subtle in its operations, and is frequently active when supposed to be wholly absent.

SECTION 5. — CONSCIENCE.

Among the springs of human action, the last and most important is **Conscience**. There is much confusion among

Conscience.

ethical writers on this subject. While the great majority agree on certain characteristics of this constituent of the soul, there are scarcely any two that agree in a complete description of it. In fact, many

Different views of different writers.

writers do not attempt a formal and comprehensive definition. The general conception most common is that of a combination of certain intellectual powers and certain sensibilities having to do with moral conduct. There is implied an intuition of

Ideas common to all.

the moral quality in actions, an exercise of the judgment as to whether certain actions are good or bad, right or wrong; an impulse to do what is judged to be right, and not to do what is judged to be wrong; a sense of approval when one has done what is judged to be right, and of degradation and condemnation when one has done what is judged to be wrong; and a sense of approval or disapproval respectively of the right or the wrong conduct of others. Sometimes all this is symbolized in the one expression *moral sense* or the *moral judgment.* It is not usually contended that Conscience as thus described always determines correctly whether a particular action is right or wrong, though some go as far as this; but for the most part, it is regarded as fallible and dependent on education.

Now, it seems to me, as it does to some others, that we may get a much more simple and definite conception of Conscience and its functions by regarding it as a wholly separate and peculiar power of the mind, standing by itself, and being in itself exclusive of any other powers of the soul. These have their distinct places and offices, and are the same when relating to moral subjects as to any other; hence we have no need to combine them with each other and with an entirely new element in order to form a Conscience. Why may not this additional element have a name and function of its own? *A separate and peculiar power.*

It would seem, then, that the most simple and unexceptionable definition of Conscience would be, that it is *that within us which impels us to do what we judge to be right, and to refrain from doing what we judge to be wrong; and which also excites in us a feeling of approval of acts which we regard as right, and of disapproval of acts which we regard as wrong.* *Definition of Conscience.*

Three cases are implied. 1. A man has in view two actions, one right and the other wrong, and having such relation to each other, that one must be performed, and the other left unperformed. He must choose between them. He cannot do both, and he cannot leave both undone. His passions or appetites may *First case.*

impel him to do the one which he knows to be wrong, and his Conscience impels him to do that which he knows to be right. It will always do this when it does anything. It is possible that the monitions of Conscience may be neglected, and so come to be disregarded and inefficient. But it still remains, if Conscience acts at all, it will be in favor of the right and against the wrong. In this respect Conscience is *infallible*, and it is only of a Conscience so defined that we can predicate infallibility.

2. The second case is of a man who has done an act of the kind described. If he has done what he judges to Second case. be right, his Conscience gives him a feeling of approval and satisfaction. If he has done what he judges to be wrong, his Conscience will make him uneasy with a feeling of disapproval and dissatisfaction.

3. It is in accordance with these conditions that we regard the conduct of others. When we see a man doing Third case. what we judge and what we know he judges to be wrong, we disapprove of his action, and are sure that if we were in his place we should have a sense of condemnation. So on the other hand, if in the face of temptation to do wrong, he has overcome and has done what he judged to be right, we approve and applaud his conduct.

The conditions, then, for the exercise of Conscience are as follows: (*a*) There must be a conception of some act Conditions to be performed. This will be by the same for the exercise of Conscience. powers of the mind as those by which other individual concepts are formed. (*b*) It must be seen to have a moral quality. The Reason or Intuition gives us this just as when the occasion occurs it gives beauty, cause and effect, power, etc. (*c*) Then the judgment decides whether the action is right or wrong. It is the same judgment that determines whether an object is small or great, hot or cold, comely or uncomely; or whether an action be wise or foolish, prudent or imprudent. It may in this case, as in other cases, err in its decision; but such as it is finally we must act upon it. (*d*) Then Conscience asserts itself. If the judgment decides that the action is right, Conscience urges to the doing of it, and if wrong to refrain from the doing of it. As we have seen, it does this always if it does anything, and is so far forth infallible. It does not compel our action; we may disregard its monition, and How far yield to some other impulse. The consequence infallible. of such action will be followed by the reproaches of Conscience, a sense of guilt and ill-desert, and an expectation of punishment.

SECTION 6. — CONFLICTING IMPULSES.

Such are the springs of human action. They have been set forth very nearly in the supposed order of their worthiness. It would be admitted by most The order of persons that the appetites are of a lower order worthiness. in this respect than the desires, and that the latter are inferior to the affections. This is not altogether true in respect to the superiority of Self-love over the Affections. Still it is not altogether false. We are to Self-love and remember that Self-love implies a desire for the Affec- one's highest individual welfare on the whole. tions. It subordinates Appetites and Desires as demanding instant gratification, to some larger and better enjoyment in the future. At the same time, it is dependent in some measure on those for its own gratification. Self-love in its narrower sense, as lapsing into selfishness, may come in conflict with the Affections, and illegitimately subordinate them. But a broad and wise Self-love in the form of Prudence may sometimes properly subordinate them, while at the same time they are a condition for its highest and noblest gratification. The indulgence of the Affections may sometimes be unworthy or inordinate, and may need, in order to the highest happiness of the individual, to be suppressed; and they may properly be cherished only under such conditions as will tend to the highest welfare. This will not be incompatible with self-denial and sacrifice for those we love, since in the exercise of those virtues the noblest pleasures of man's being consist.

But Self-love, as we have seen, may become inordinate and vicious, and thus may need some check. Here it Self-love in comes in conflict with Conscience; and Conscience with science must have the right of way, and be the Conscience. supreme and dominant impulse in the soul.

Let us illustrate these conflicts by some single instances. Here is a man who craves some article of food or drink, Illustration. not because he is hungry or thirsty, but because it will pleasantly affect the organs of physical taste. The money which he would spend for this will purchase for him a book, or admit him to a lecture, or gratify some other desire of the mind. Here Desire is in conflict with Appetite, and it is not difficult to determine which of these is the worthier impulse, and therefore making the higher demand. But suppose further, there is a friend who is in trouble, and whom a small amount of money would relieve. This claim would be higher than that of mere Desire. It may be, however, that the friend has committed a crime, and his trouble is that he is likely to suffer a just penalty, and that the crime is one against my own rights of life and property, and that his deliverance from punishment is likely to result in its repetition ; then Prudence would be and should be superior to Affection, and induce me to let justice take its course.

But Self-love, as has been intimated, may come in conflict with Conscience. We may not seek our own happiness where it involves the violation of some moral law, even where no Appetite, or Desire, or Affection is concerned. Here Conscience is paramount, and Self-love must be subordinate. It is also evident that Conscience may come in conflict with each of the lower impulses, as well as that of Self-love. It may demand that the indulgence of Appetite, where such indulgence would harm health, or involve much waste, should be suppressed. It may also require that the gratification of Desire, if it impels to what is hurtful, should be refused. It may be that not only the Malevolent Affections, but some inordinate Benevolent Affections, should be restrained because threatening to eventuate in unrighteousness. It must thus rule all along the line. It is the most authoritative impulse of the soul ; and when *authority*, however weak, conflicts with any mere *strength*, however great, the latter must give way and the former prevail. Supremacy of Conscience.

That Conscience is thus supremely authoritative is further evident from several considerations. In the first place, it may be easily shown that man's highest welfare is secured by yielding to this as the paramount authority. The Appetites and Passions, when acting in subordination to Self-love, clearly Evident from several considerations.

produce a larger amount of happiness than when permitted to indulge themselves without restraint. We all know that unlimited gratification results in such disorder of these impulses, that they become causes of misery rather than enjoyment; while a moderate and restricted use, or temporary suppression of them results in a larger measure of enjoyment in the future. So, too, when Self-love antagonizes Conscience, the man who yields to the authority of the latter not only secures all the happiness that he would in obeying the sole impulse of Self-love, but a purer and nobler enjoyment in the consciousness that he has done the more fit and manlier thing, and in freedom from the sense of degradation that comes from yielding to a baser motive.

Then, again, the man who obeys Conscience is always sure that he is actuated by the highest possible principle, **Broad and comprehensive Self-love may coincide with Conscience.** and is building up a worthy and righteous character. It is true that a broad and comprehensive Self-love, if we had intelligence enough to see what would be for our highest good, might, and probably would, impel to the very same conduct to which Conscience would urge, and that the results would be coincident. But we are not omniscient, and Self-love will impel us to such acts as seem to us for our highest welfare, whether they really are or not; and for this reason Self-love and Conscience will frequently be in conflict. In other words, if we always knew just what is right, expediency would doubtless demand the doing of it; but as we do not know with perfect accuracy always either the right or the expedient, what seems to us to be these are liable to be in conflict.

But suppose it were possible that Self-love would

prompt only to that which is right, yet even so there would be a difference to ourselves between acts done under this impulse and those done under the impulse of Conscience. We should feel that we had acted more worthily in the latter case than in the former, though the results otherwise might be the same. Almost anyone will admit the moral superiority of actions done because they are right, over precisely the same actions done because they will increase our personal enjoyment.

A Difference between acting from Self-love as a motive, and from Conscience, even when not antagonistic.

CHAPTER IV.

VIRTUE.

SECTION 1. — THE NATURE OF VIRTUE.

THE term **Virtue** has been used heretofore in our discussions in the general and popular sense of moral excellence, or of conduct such as the intelligent conscience approves. But it needs to be more particularly and scientifically understood.

The word itself is from the Latin *virtus;* and this is derived from *vir*, the Latin term, not for a human being, but for one who is more emphatically *a man*, having something of the nobler and more heroic type. Thus it is easy to see how, originally, it meant all that is implied in our word "manliness," and perhaps something more. It had reference especially to military prowess, including the qualities of courage, energy, obedience at whatever sacrifice, orderliness, fortitude, and unswerving loyalty. From this meaning the transition was easy to that of the moral contest to which man is exposed. Qualities similar to those just enumerated are implied where one, under the influence of temptation, whether of outward allurements or inward impulses, still persists in obedience to the law of righteousness. There is a call in the contest here implied for courage, energy,

Original meaning of Virtue.

decision of character, independence, loyalty, self-forgetful-
ness, sacrifice, and whatever pertains to the highest manliness. Nobility and greatness of character were never
displayed on the battlefield, or in any physical exploit,
which were superior to similar characteristics shown by
men and women who, in the midst of fierce temptations,
have been true to their convictions, and steadfast in their
obedience to moral principle.

Here a question arises which has interested many minds,
namely, whether there can be any virtue where there is
no temptation to do wrong. It has already Can there be
been implied in the previous discussions that Virtue where
there is no
there is no virtue where there is no possibility Temptation?
of doing wrong. But under the law of habit, as has been
shown, it is possible for a human being to arrive at such
a position that there is no longer any consciousness of
temptation, because all desires for whatever involves evil
have been extirpated, and the soul craves only what is
morally right. Now, the action of such a person may
properly be called virtuous, not simply because he never
does wrong and always does right, but because he has,
through contests, and the putting forth of energies, and
in the exercise of self-denials, and through sacrifices,
achieved this condition. It is the result of conflicts
valiantly waged and successfully accomplished. Therefore his present state may rightly be regarded as virtuous.

Nevertheless, one may be permitted to believe that
not all moral excellence is virtue in its highest or in its
strictest sense. It is evident that we instinc- Not all moral
tively estimate the degree of virtue by the Excellence to
be regarded
greater or less degree of inducement to the as Virtue.
contrary; and where there is an absence of such induce-

ment we can hardly consider it as virtue at all. Dr. Peabody says that we do not think of attributing virtue to a child not come to years of accountability, notwithstanding it may have many beautiful traits of character, and great innocence and amiability. But there may be certain characteristics of adults which have no taint of vice in them, but which are still not virtuous. Some persons have a quiet, dull constitution; and their freedom from wickedness is not from the power of moral principle, but from lack of energy. A very lazy man is free from certain vices into which an energetic, restless man is likely to fall. Then, again, men are free from certain vices simply from want of opportunity. Their environment has been such as to preclude certain inducements to do wrong. It is often the case that a man who has sustained a good character for years, even till middle life, or verging upon old age, suddenly falls into wrong-doing. It is not that all his life before was one of superior virtue, and that he has all at once become vicious, but he has come into what are to him unprecedented conditions; and the propensity which till now has had nothing to call it into action, though existing in all its latent power, is suddenly awakened, and the man falls an easy prey.

Virtue, then, may be defined as *conformity to the moral law*, or obedience to Conscience as the impulse to do what **Definition.** we judge to be right, and to refrain from what we judge to be wrong, where there is, or has been, opportunity, and more or less inducement, to do the opposite.

These terms obviously have not the same signification, though a clear discrimination is not always made in the use of them. **Piety, or Religion,** has reference to the relations of the soul to God, and the obligations growing out of those relations. **Virtue** has reference to all kinds of moral relations and obligations. It is conceivable that a sceptic, or even an atheist, may be virtuous, though, by the very nature of the case, destitute of piety. He may recognize his relations to his fellow-men, and that certain duties arise therefrom; and he may discharge all the obligations herein implied. I do not undertake now to discuss the question whether this unbelief in God comes from a neglect of using means of information which he was under obligation to use, or, in other words, whether there are any honest sceptics and atheists. This is at least conceivable, that such persons may be virtuous, though not religious. Most of us have known some such unbelievers whose moral character, as distinguished from their religious character, was without reproach.

But there is a sense in which Virtue implies Religion; and, on the other hand, there is a sense in which Religion, or Piety, implies Virtue. Virtue, as we have seen, consists in obedience to the moral law, as far as it is or may be known. This applies to our relations to all beings in the universe with whom we are brought into any kind of moral relations. Now, we are in relations with God of a most intimate and solemn character. We are bound to act in moral accordance with these relations. To do so is Virtue, and not to do so is the contrary of Virtue. Hence to those who know their relations to God, and refuse to act in accordance with these relations, we cannot attribute virtuous conduct. To such to be not religious is to be not virtuous.

On the other hand, a religious person must be virtuous. There are those who deny this, and hold that morality and **Piety implies** piety are quite independent of each other. It **Virtue.** is true they are not the same; yet since, as we have had occasion to see, the moral law is also the law of God, and as to be religious implies the doing of the will of God, no vicious or immoral person can be regarded as a pious person. The converse of this is not true in so far as it is conceivable that one may be ignorant of God and all relations to him. On the whole, it may be said that Virtue is a broader term than Piety, and that Piety itself is a Virtue.

SECTION 3. — THE VIRTUES.

Heretofore Virtue has been spoken of as a characteristic of the soul, and it is in this sense one and indivisible. **Virtue as a** It consists in a settled purpose or general dis- **quality of** position to conform to the law of right, and to **the Soul.** obey conscience. But it has many forms of manifestation; and these forms take on the names of Virtues. Attempts have been made to form these into **Groups of** groups, but with indifferent success. There **Virtues.** is danger in such a division that some kinds of conduct may be regarded as virtues which are not virtues; as, for instance, **Prudence** is by many writers **Is Prudence** regarded as a virtue. In a certain sense, and **a Virtue?** by an accommodation of language, this may be allowable; but in strict propriety it is not so. It may be our duty to be prudent, — and imprudence is certainly sometimes a vice, — but prudence may be practised from the mere impulse of self-love, with no thought of moral principle connected with it. It is prudent for a man to protect himself from the cold in a severe day by wearing an overcoat; but he protects himself for his own comfort, and for his own health's sake, and not because the act has any moral character. A man may put up an umbrella when it rains, but that is not necessarily a virtuous act. It is true we may do the same things at one time under the impulse of Conscience that we do at another from Self-love. In the one case it is a virtue: in the other it is not.

Fortitude is usually regarded as a virtue. It is undoubtedly a worthy trait of character; and the person who is wholly destitute of it, or who has it in only a small degree, can but stand lower, both in his own respect and in the respect of his fellow-men, than if he had it. It may be a virtue, and that, too, of high rank; still, it is not necessarily so. The savage Indian, captured by his savage foes, and subjected to the most excruciating torture, bears with the greatest equanimity the utmost that can be done to him, even sometimes taunting his tormentors with the tameness of their inventions; but this may be from an impulse of pride, and not from any moral principle. There are many other worthy and excellent traits of character which are so akin to the virtues as to be commonly reckoned among them, but which, nevertheless, so far differ from them that they must be regarded as really something else, and only come up to the grade of virtues when the motive to them is of a purely moral character.

Fortitude a Virtue, but not always or necessarily.

The second part of this volume will set forth the various virtues which pertain to men governed by moral principles.

BOOK II.

PRACTICAL ETHICS.

51

PRELIMINARY CHAPTER.

DIVISION OF THE SUBJECT.

PRACTICAL Ethics comprises the application of the principles developed in Theoretical Ethics, and also a classification and explanation of the various duties Classes of involved. These duties are naturally divided Duties. into three groups, and will be treated under the following heads : —

Part I. Duties to Self.

Part II. Duties to our Fellow-men :
  Division I. Justice.
    Class 1. Domestic Duties.
    Class 2. Duties to Individuals.
    Class 3. Duties to Society.
  Division II. Beneficence.

Part III. Duties to God.

All duties are primarily due to God as being our Creator, and therefore having a supreme claim on all our powers of service of every sort. He has also instituted the relations between us and all other beings ; and consequently the obligations which spring out of these relations are of Divine ordinance, and therefore binding upon us. It is true, that, if we could conceive of ourselves as having no such relations to God, but only our present relations to other beings, there would still be duties implied in these relations.   Hence there is a double obligation : we are to treat our fellow-man righteously because he is our fellow-

Double
Obligation
towards our
Fellow-men.
man, and also because God, for reasons of his own, requires it of us, as he would have a right to require it even if we had no perception of the relations between us and them.

For these reasons the natural order of presentation would be to begin with the duties we owe to God, or Religious Ethics.   But as we learn largely through expe-rience our duties and obligations, and as we naturally begin with what is nearest to us, it is thought best to follow the order of development thus implied rather than the other order.

PART I.

DUTIES TO SELF.

55

GENERAL DUTY OF SELF–CULTURE.

THE ultimate of all duty implied here is that of acquiring a perfectly worthy character. All other duties to self are subsidiary to this. Indeed, it may be said **The great** that all other duties of every sort contribute to **End of all** this, whether this be the immediate object or **Duty to Self.** not. To have a pure, strong, symmetrical, and attractive character, is immeasurably superior to all other wealth and all other good, and, we may well say, is the chief end of man's existence. But in this, as in all other great achievements, there is implied a great variety of methods and operations. These we shall consider in order.

CHAPTER I.

DUTIES TO THE BODY.

IT may seem to superficial thinkers that attention to a material and temporary organism hardly deserves to be reckoned among ethical duties. But, if we **Importance** carefully consider the subject, we shall see that **of Duties to** these duties, even if last in importance, are first **the Body.** in the order of time. Clearly enough, as under our present constitution a properly trained body is a condition for the effective action of the soul, before all things we must bestow a certain kind and amount of care upon it. If no care be taken of the body the soul will be crippled and enfeebled in its activities. The desirableness that this one great instrument of the soul should, as nearly as possible, approximate perfection, is too obvious for discussion.

SECTION 1. — SUBSISTENCE.

The first duty we owe our bodies is to providé the things essential to their **subsistence**. The body must have nourishment to supply the waste of its tissues constantly taking place. It must also have raiment and shelter suitable to preserve it from the effects of varying temperature, and other conditions to which it is constantly exposed. Provision of these kinds implies many others which easily suggest themselves.

The great leading virtue here involved is **Industry**. Productive labor is the duty of every man, unless in some The virtue of way incapacitated for it. Nature abundantly Industry. furnishes the materials to supply human waste; but they are not available without human labor. This duty of industry is universal. In its broad sense there is *no laboring class.* Every able-bodied man, who is also This duty mentally competent, is under obligation to pro- universal. duce, at least, as much as he consumes. In- herited wealth furnishes no exemption from this obligation. It is one of the evils of modern society, as it doubtless was of ancient, that men who are rich, and are not com- pelled by fear of want to labor, think that, therefore, they have no such duty. This is a great mistake, and very many of the moral and economic evils of our times come from it. Wealth, like many another gift of Providence, brings with it its responsibilities, and among these is the duty of using this wealth in such a manner as will be productive of the greatest good to the community. This cannot well be accomplished unless the owner give himself to some kind of labor of body or mind. By this is not meant that every man should engage in business enterprises, or that one should not under certain circumstances retire from business. But he has no right to be indolent, or refuse to occupy himself with work that will be beneficial to the community generally.

Duties imposed by Wealth.

It is doubtless a blessing to humanity that men's wants are made the occasion for labor, since but for this motive most men would never do any protracted, systematic work. But it is a crying evil that there are men who live on the wealth of their ancestors, and add nothing to the wealth of the community.

Here we may properly consider the duty of securing a competence for the future. If it be the duty of a man to produce by his labor those commodities or their equivalent, the consumption of which is a condition of his continued temporal existence, plainly this duty is not limited by his present daily needs. In the life of every person there are likely to come days and months and possibly years, when he cannot labor. It is his duty as far as practicable to provide beforehand for these emergencies. It is true some cannot do this. There are those whose powers of body or mind are too feeble to achieve more than the supply for each day as it comes, and the supply is often scanty at that. But it is practicable for a large proportion of men, not only to produce what they

Duty to provide for the future.

consume as they go along, but while they have their health and strength to produce more than they consume. The virtues here implied are those of **diligence**, **frugality**,

Virtues implied here. and **economy**, though the last term has a broader signification than would be assigned to it in the present connection. Like some other virtues it implies more or less of temporary self-denial and sacrifice. But it may be prompted by self-love, and may stop short of a moral virtue. It is, nevertheless, a duty as well as a policy of prudence.

The call for *self-denial* here comes from the conflict of the appetites and the desires both with the demand of self-love and that of conscience. There are so many cravings for instant gratification, the most positive dictates of prudence are overcome, while the voice of duty is wholly unheard. Yet there are moments when it is heard above both the clamorings of passion and the demands of selfishness. Not all the poverty in the world comes from disregard of the duties of industry, frugality, and economy, but unquestionably a great part of it is due to this.

To what extent frugality should be carried is a question of some interest. There may be a saving that is incon-

Extent to which frugality should be carried. sistent with economy. When one denies to one's self what is essential to the preservation of vigor, and for the sake of accumulation partakes of insufficient and innutritious food, and is clad with rags, or lives in a filthy den instead of a comfortable, even if a humble dwelling, one becomes either incompetent to produce, or settles into the wretched condition of a miser, whose character and state are fitly indicated by the term itself.

Is there a moral justification of the accumulation of great fortunes? There has been in the past, as there is in the present, so much of injustice and fraud, so much of advantage taken of the less shrewd and more scrupulous by the more shrewd and less scrupulous in the acquisition of wealth, and so much of vain and vulgar display and wanton wastefulness in its use, that many good people have an uncomfortable feeling in the contemplation of great riches. But surely wealth acquired by legitimate means is not a necessary evil, either to its possessor or to the community. By legitimate means is implied generally that this wealth is really produced by the possessor of it. That one person may be able to produce five, ten, twenty, or even a hundred times as much as another, and that, too, without subtracting from another's share, but rather helping the accumulation of others, is as obvious as that one man may have greater physical strength or more mental power than another. It would seem that to a man who has this gift of producing much wealth, no matter how much, such production is not only permissible but obligatory. The more wealth there is in the community, provided it is not unjustly obtained or improperly used, the better it is for the community.

Wealth not a necessary evil.

In the present state of human society there must be great capitals for the operation of business enterprises on a scale that will supply the wants of men. With the steady and rapid increase of population in all civilized nations, but for these vast productive agencies which would be impossible but for great accumulations of capital, population would soon trench upon production, and there would be an immense

Great capitals necessary.

increase of poverty and suffering. These accumulations could not take place under our present social system, except by the efforts and enterprise of individuals endowed with unusual business ability. This, doubtless, has very much to do with our relations to our fellow-men, and involves certain duties to them. But it also concerns our duties to ourselves.

SECTION 2. — HEALTH.

A sound body is of inestimable importance to every man. As an instrument of the soul, and a condition for its effective action, we need to make it and keep it as nearly perfect as possible. As previously remarked, a weak, sickly, crippled body is an incalculable detriment to the mind. It is true, there have been instances of persons with feeble bodies who have yet been wonderfully efficient in the world. Of some of these the influence has been far-reaching in their own generation, and has perpetuated itself in the subsequent ages. But these are exceptional instances; only a very few have been able to overcome their physical disadvantages, and they were persons of extraordinary mental endowments. It is something of an argument against the materialistic philosophy that there have been such minds, and that they have been so far superior to physical conditions as to indicate that mind is not a mere function of matter. It is evidently superior to the body, and uses the latter simply as its instrument; and some minds with very poor instruments can achieve more than others with good ones.

Physical vigor essential.

The duties we owe to the body in respect to health, are partly implied in what has already been set forth under the head of subsistence. There must be suitable and

sufficient food, raiment, and shelter, not only that the body
may be kept alive, but that it may be kept in health. Industry, diligence, and the careful calculation   The duty of
which is implied in economy, are essential to   Health.
this end. Some fail in these respects through sheer indolence, and others through various self-indulgences, or
by exchanging the produce of their labor for that which
does not meet their wants.

To this end men must also cultivate **Temperance**. I do
not use the term here in its popular sense of abstinence
from intoxicating beverages. Abstinence, not   Proper
only from these, but from certain other objects   meaning of
of appetite, is a duty. But the word is used   Temperance.
here in the broad sense of restraining one's appetites
within their proper limits. Men are tempted to eat and
drink, not only what is wholesome and invigorating, but
what is harmful and enfeebling. Even many things which,
when received in reasonable quantities, are nourishing and
healthful, may be partaken of so largely as to more than
neutralize the good effect they would normally produce.
So men become gluttons and gormandizers, and breed
various diseases and distempers of the body.

In order to the perfection of the physical powers, one
must exercise steady control over the appetites. This is
not a difficult matter when these propensities have not
been indulged so far as to grow into tyrannical habits.
But when the latter is the case, the effort and   Control of
care required are very great, and to many a poor   the appetites
victim it seems well-nigh hopeless. It is so   not difficult.
much easier when we once have the mastery to retain it
than to regain it when we have lost it, that one needs to
beware how he relaxes his vigilance. There are multitudes

of physical wrecks in our communities; and to a very large extent these are the results of intemperance in the sense of immoderate use of such things as are good in themselves, or, it may be, indispensable within their proper limits. There are other multitudes who, while not wrecks, still lack much that belongs to manly vigor and power.

Consequences of intemperance.

It should be noted that we are not now insisting on health merely in the sense that there is an absence of positive disease. That is but a kind of negative physical condition. There may be, and it is our business to see that there is, over and above this, an abounding vitality, an energy, and an elasticity, which multiply one's effectiveness many fold. In order to this, there must be in addition to the conditions already mentioned several others. Both men and women need to have an eye to sanitary effect in the matter of **Dress**. There is a vulgar and slangy expression when persons are spoken of as "dressed to kill," which might well be wrested from its disreputable connections, and put to a sober and sensible use, for I fear it indicates a very unpleasant truth about a considerable number of persons.

Moral relation of Dress.

Another duty is that of **Cleanliness**. This is so obvious that it becomes almost offensive to speak of it, as though there might be some lack in this respect. Surely there is no call, as most men are situated, to be economical in the use of water. It is scarcely of more importance as a matter of decency than as a condition for physical health. A large part of the Old Testament religious ceremonial regimen consists of directions for washings and cleansings of the body. Many other ancient religions lay much stress on this.

The generous use of water.

Physical purity is no doubt intended to symbolize spiritual and inward purity. But it is none the less a very great virtue in itself.

There is a whole group of duties somewhat closely affiliated but not of inferior importance. A certain amount of **Sleep** is absolutely essential to the best physical condition. That it should occur at regular intervals, and as far as possible be undisturbed, is obvious. The constitution of things is happily such as to conspire to this end. The night when men cannot work to advantage, and when in a well-ordered community business largely ceases, and there are peace and quiet, is evidently the time for sleep. It is unfortunate when either the customs of society or individual habits turn night into day or the reverse.

There must be periods of **Rest** and this aside from sleep. These are not necessarily times of idleness or vacuity, but opportunities for the mind and body to relax themselves and give way to spontaneous activity within the limits of one's own physical welfare and the liberties and privileges of others. To persons of sedentary occupation this may be coincident with **Physical exercise** and **Recreation.** Play in the proper sense of that term, when the faculties unbend themselves and are released from their ordinary strains and allowed to act more freely, giving a certain zest and exhilaration to the mind, is almost indispensable to a large number of persons. There are doubtless few among the young who need exhortation to this as a duty; yet these few by refraining from relaxation do great damage to their physical constitution.

Finally, **Regularity of habits** is among the chief utilities tending to physical welfare. To have our hours for work, for sleep, for exercise, for society, for meditation, for eating, and for resting, to order our lives on some well-digested plan, tends powerfully to sound health and the prolongation of life. It is true there is a possibility of going to an extreme in this attempt to live by rule.

Important functions of impulse. Some have laid down for themselves such minute regulations that they have left no room for the play of **healthy impulse.** And yet our impulses are a part of our constitution and have an office to perform. To shut them out from all part in the government of our lives is to ignore Providence, set up an arbitrary system, and do ourselves much harm. To know all the conditions on which physical prosperity depends is not given to man. Hence we must depend, to a certain extent, upon certain instinctive impulses which are given us for a wise purpose. They are to be kept subordinate, but they are not useless. In a man of perfectly healthy soul and body their action is likely to coincide with the decision of sound reason.

SECTION 3. — PERSONAL APPEARANCE.

Among our duties to ourselves is certainly included some attention to our **Personal appearance.** It cannot be a matter of indifference from a moral point of view whether we are personally agreeable or disagreeable to others. That we are under obligation to rid ourselves, as far as possible, of whatever tends to the latter condition and to cultivate whatever tends to the former, is fairly evident on the face of it. It is true that not every one has physical beauty, either of face or of form. But most can keep themselves from being offensive and repulsive. An individual may be plain or even deformed, and yet win respect and approval by cultivating certain physical virtues. Among these are neatness, good taste, skilful management of the body, and the avoidance of Cultivation the opposite of these, as negligence, carelessness, of this char-slovenliness, and slouching, clownish habits. acteristic.

One need not be a "dandy" or a "dude;" indeed, the qualities implied in these terms are to be avoided quite as much as those just previously mentioned; but every one may have and should have good manners (and good morals include these), a certain dignity and self-respect, a sense of propriety, and a mingling of gentleness and manliness. These are all elements of inestimable personal value.

SECTION 4. — CHASTITY.

This subject pertains not more to the welfare of the body than to the moral health of the soul, but it may perhaps be better considered here than elsewhere. It is all Reasons for the more of vital importance because of its seclu- its consider-sion from the range of general discussion by its ation here. very nature, and by the fact that its violation is among the secret vices into which so many are liable to fall.

The consequences of incontinence to the body are of the most damaging character. It generates the foulest diseases and makes miserable wrecks of thousands of men and women. It saps the foundation of all manly vigor and mightily diminishes all power of usefulness. In communities where it is most prevalent a physically feeble and puny race is the consequence.

The effect on the mind is still more disastrous. Indulgence is preceded by unworthy and base thoughts and impure imaginations, always tending more and more to familiarize the subject with vice, and to reconcile one to its naturally repulsive features. Nothing is more destruc-

Effect on the mind. tive of mental vigor, of refined and delicate sensibilities, and of spiritual vitality, than sensual conduct and the indulgence of the imagination in impure conceptions. The mind under such perverted culture becomes a nest of filthy abominations, from which at last the wretched victim would fly if it were possible to escape.

Its influence on the community is incalculably evil. If

Effect on the community. generally indulged, the disorder and wretchedness would be appalling. Homes there would be none, families would be broken up, children would be cared for only by the public, and the whole moral structure of society would tend to utter dissolution.

Finally, it would be a moral and religious evil of the most calamitous character. No personal duty is more clearly indicated by natural religion, and more frequently and explicitly set forth in the Bible, than that of Chastity. To disregard its obligations is more palpable rebellion against the Divine authority and the Divine government than is found in almost any other sin. All considerations, moral, religious, social, personal, and prudential, cry out with a loud voice to every young person, "Keep thyself pure."

CHAPTER II.

DUTIES TO THE MIND.

IN general, our duty to the mind is to make it as effective and powerful as possible in all its depart- General ments. It is not possible for every one to give duty. a very large proportion of time to mental culture, but a certain amount can be given even by the least favored; many are so situated that this will coincide with their main business. In order to the achievement of great mental strength there must be an harmonious development of the several faculties and powers. There is in our times, as perhaps there has been in all times, a tendency to one-sided mental development, certain powers being cultivated to the neglect of others. Thus there has been and is a want of proportion and symmetry, a lack of balance and therefore of effectiveness.

SECTION 1. — DUTIES TO THE INTELLECT.

As the body is a condition for the action of the soul generally, so is the Intellect a condition for the action of the Sensibilities and the Will. As a condition it Relation of is lower in importance than these, being in the Intellect, relation to them as means to an end. For, how- and Will. ever true it may be that intellectual exercise is itself a satisfaction, yet this satisfaction can only exist as the Sensibilities are affected by the knowledge. It is the business of the Intellect to perceive, to reason, to imagine, to investigate, and, finally, to know.[1]

At the beginning of this discussion of Duties to one's self, it was laid down as a general obligation, embracing all others, to acquire a perfect character. Evidently ignorance would imply a very great imperfection. It is, therefore, a duty to secure knowledge. To this end there must be much training and discipline of the faculties. We must not only know how to read intelligently, and to take in oral discourse, but to observe, to compare, to discriminate, to judge correctly, to generalize, and to think deeply and widely. Some men can devote much time to this intellectual culture; and it is their duty to use their opportunity to its utmost extent. The majority of men have not so much time to devote to this purpose, but all have the means of securing a certain amount of knowledge; and by using diligently such means as they have, by keeping eyes and ears open, by improving all opportunities to gain information, they will prove that gross ignorance is not a necessity.

Mental training and discipline.

But it is not knowledge, nor learning alone, that is the end of this duty. There are many learned men who yet lack wisdom; and we have high authority for asserting that "Wisdom is the principal thing." Wisdom is the ability to adapt means to ends, to apprehend the signification of things which are observed, and to estimate their relative value and utility. It ascertains sometimes at a glance the nature of a difficulty, and discerns its solution. It is nearly synonymous with good judgment, and, when found among the un-

Wisdom as well as Learning necessary.

[1] Dr. Hopkins's Outline Study of Man.

learned or uneducated, as it not unfrequently is, it goes by the name of **common sense.**

To have a fair share of the qualities implied in this ability is to have valuable elements of character; and there are few that need to be destitute of this fair share, if they will take the trouble to seek it. To be without it implies a certain moral as well as intellectual poverty, and a lack of energy and enterprise that is not justifiable.

But it is our duty not merely to get Knowledge and Wisdom, but to get **Power.** The intellect is an instrument, and as such it should be made as perfect as possible. Every man is a member of society; and it is the duty of each member to contribute, not simply what may be called "his share," but *as much as he can*, to the common weal. God has made each individual for some particu- The Highest lar purpose, and has endowed him with the rudi- Power to be mentary means by the development of which he sought. may the most completely effect that purpose. Some men have natural ability for the pursuits of science; and among the sciences one may be fitted for a mathematician, another to be an adept in Chemistry or Biology, and another in Natural History. In other lines one may be adapted to philosophy, and one to literature, or to oratory, or history; still others find their congenial fields in business, or exploration, or in politics. It is for each to cultivate the gift that is in him, to become a man of as much power as possible. In this way only will each one fulfil his own vocation, and attain to the wealth of character which he owes to himself; and the community will be richer and mightier than would otherwise be possible.

I have not undertaken to speak of the separate powers of the intellect; but there is one to which it may be well to devote a brief space. The **Imagination** is a faculty of the mind which, while looked upon by some as ornamental Utility of the rather than useful, and by others as though Imagination. wholly idle and unreal, is nevertheless of vast benefit and great importance in its moral bearings. Imagination is the power to combine conceptions into new wholes, and to modify these at pleasure. It deals not with the real but with the ideal. It is of value in forming plans of projects to be accomplished, or at least to be considered. It is essential to invention, since the inventor needs to have the idea of that which he is preparing in his mind so that he can change it, or adapt it to its uses, and determine its proportions and necessary elements. It is not confined in this respect to mechanical contrivances: it has to do with thoughts and schemes of thoughts which are to be developed into treatises, and with hypotheses which are to be tested by scientific investigation. It also has much to do with scenes which it may conjure up or construct, and on which it delights to dwell.

Here is where its moral influence becomes palpable. We may form images and pictures of pure or of impure Its Moral things in our minds. There are certain combi-Value. nations and representations on which one delights to dwell; and he encourages these, and keeps them in mind, and recalls them in moments of leisure. It depends very much on the character of these representations what the character of the subject of them shall be. If he delights in representations of noble, elevating, and clear conceptions, these will come into his mind, and will be welcomed there; and he will be made by the contemplation of them nobler, purer, and more worthy. If, on the other hand, he is accustomed to bring before his mind images of impurity, and representations of vicious enjoyments, even though he commits no overt vicious act, he is still preparing himself, by the corruption of his soul, for evil practice, into which he will easily fall when the temptation presents himself.

The moral uses of imagination are seen again in bringing before the mind ideals of moral goodness and exalted worth. In nearly all our plans of life, secular as well as religious, we set before us consciously or unconsciously some ideal which all strive with more or less earnestness to realize. One young man has in his mind that he will be a man of science, another will take the line of literature, another of business; and each sets before his mind, and holds in his imagination, the kind of person in several respects that he means to become. So, in the formation of moral character: a young man has something of an ideal of the character which he hopes to realize. It may be a low and unworthy one, or a high and noble and yet imperfect, one; but the higher and better it is, the more likely he is to become an upright, honorable, and reputable person. These ideals have an incalculable influence on character and destiny.

The Advantage of moral ideals.

SECTION 2. — THE SENSIBILITIES.

A man's duties in this region of his personality are not perhaps at first glance so obvious as they are elsewhere, but they are not less real. It is here that the great springs of character are found; and if these be properly regulated and subjected to the law of righteousness, all other powers are likely to rightly order themselves.

Importance of our duty to our Sensibilities.

Using the term **Desires** in the broad sense as covering all the cravings of the soul, we shall easily see that the great general duty concerning our sensibilities is to keep them within their normal limits, and at the same time in their full vigor. We have already learned that the duties we owe to our bodies include the control and proper discipline of the appetites. Our duties to the mind involve the training and chastening of all the other desires. If we carefully observe the development of our own character, we shall find that, especially at an undisciplined stage of development, there are desires for certain improper things. There is also a lack of desire for certain things that are proper, and even essential to the welfare of the person. Again, we find some desires even for things useful and profitable that are too strong, and others that are too weak. On the one hand there is an obligation to create and to strengthen desire, and on the other to

Difficulty of controlling the Sensibilities. diminish and suppress it. The apparent difficulty here is in the fact that the desires are under the control of natural law, and not subject to the direct action of the Will. But, as we have seen, though the will cannot *directly* create or increase a desire, nor the contrary, it can do so *indirectly*. Desire grows by being gratified, and is weakened, and may be finally extirpated, by being denied gratification. We may also ply ourselves with motives so that desires will spring up which previously did not exist, and will grow weak

Ability to control our environment. and diminish where exciting motives are removed. In other words, though environment forms a powerful influence in the creation of character, environment may be modified or wholly changed.

But the great characteristic of moral disorder in the

sensibilities is the fact of **antagonistic desires** and impulses. There are cravings for things which are incompatible with each other: to gratify one is to refuse grati- Antagonistic fication to another. The child wishes to eat desires. his cake to-day, and also wishes to keep it till to-morrow. To do the one is to render the other impossible. A young woman has earned a sum of money by labor of some kind. She desires to use it in purchasing a gold watch. She also desires to expend it for a term at an academy. She cannot do both. A young man has reached a certain stage in the indulgence of his appetite. He wishes to drink with his boon companions, or, possibly, by himself. He also wishes to be regarded as a sober, temperate, and re- spectable person. He is convinced that he cannot gratify both of these desires. To gratify one is to deny the other. So we shall find that there may be two, three, or four sets of conflicting desires in the same mind at the same time. The problem is to harmonize these desires so that there will be no conflict. This would be a condition of complete liberty as well as of entire peace, whereas the other is that of restraint, bondage, and contest: of not having what one wants, and having a great many things that he does not want. Such a state must be one of unhappiness. The only method of emancipation is to discipline the desires so that they shall be in harmony. When we come to desire only what is right and proper, — to desire all things that we ought to have, — then our desires will have no longer conflict; then we shall have whatever we desire, and we shall have nothing we do not desire.

This is the state of perfect personal freedom. It may be illustrated by the accompanying diagram. We have first the line A, of perfect rectitude, representing what a theist would call the Divine desire, which would of course imply the Divine will. We have in the figure B a congeries of

The attainment of complete personal Liberty.

lines crossing and antagonizing one another in all sorts of ways, — a state of conflict and confusion, the condition of an untrained and undisciplined human soul. The remedy for this evil condition is,

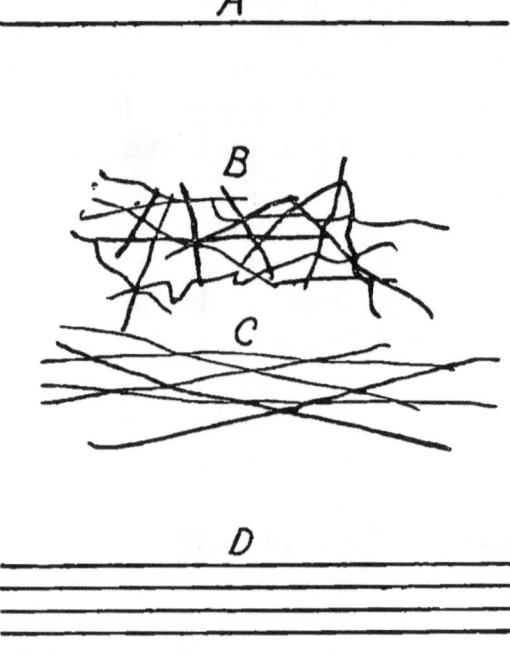

as previously remarked, to get these lines of desire to run in the same direction, — that is, parallel with each other. This can be accomplished by getting each to run parallel with the Divine desire; then, according to the familiar axiom, they must run parallel with each other.

The third figure, C, represents an effort to train the desires in the direction indicated. There is still more or less conflict, but there is improvement. This is the condition of a large proportion of persons whom we know. In the fourth figure, D, we have the training completed; each desire runs parallel with the Divine standard line. All antagonism has ceased. The soul desires nothing it cannot have; it has nothing it does not desire. It has become adjusted to the eternal laws, and is at peace, and in the infinite liberty of the truth.

It is furthermore incumbent on us to cultivate our **Esthetic feelings.** Good Taste, a delight in beauty, and avoidance of what is intrinsically repulsive, **Esthetic culture.** provided it does not arise from unavoidable conditions, these appertain to a perfect character, and are to be cultivated, though in subordination to other duties. We cannot all be great artists any more than we can be great scholars, or possess great wealth, or great genius; but we may all cultivate a love for what is beautiful; and good taste is wholly compatible with good sense.

It is also our duty to possess a **cheerful spirit.** To be always gloomy or morose, to look upon the **A cheerful disposition.** dark side of things, to make ourselves unhappy by magnifying and multiplying the evils with which we come in contact, is to subtract much from the value of character and the joy of living. It is true that this, like many another virtue, may be carried to excess and thus become a fault. One may be frivolous and trifling, and so become superficial and thoughtless. But a genuinely cheerful disposition, looking upon the pleasant side of even the ills of life, always finding something to be thankful for, is not only compatible with a sober, sensible, and deeply earnest character, but it is something to be sought for and cherished with great diligence.

Not the least among the duties to the sensibilities is the cultivation of a quick and sensitive Conscience. If what has been said concerning the conscience in another place is substantially correct, its seat is here in the sensibilities, and it is the most authoritative of all our impulses. We have seen that it always impels us to do what we judge to be right, and restrains us from what we judge to be wrong. We have nothing to do in the training of the conscience in this respect as if it might do the opposite and so need rectification. If it does anything, it does this, and not something inconsistent with it. We may love or hate what we ought not to; our desires and appetites may crave what they should not, and this abnormal action we need to be able to change by such means as we have seen to be practicable; but the Conscience never prompts us to do what we judge to be wrong, and so in this respect needs no change. But while the Conscience always impels in the right direction, if at all, it may become weak and inefficient through neglect and inattention. When men who have begun to disregard the voice of Conscience persist in this bad usage, that voice will to their apprehension grow weaker and weaker till possibly it ceases to have any effect on the evil-doer. It is a lamentable loss to human character when the voice of this inward monitor becomes deadened even in a moderate degree; how much more when it virtually becomes altogether silent. The duty here then, evidently, is to keep the Conscience quick and tender, to treat its slightest warning with attention, to obey its every behest. In this way, and in this way only, will one come to have a healthy moral character and a steady defence against all practical evils.

Character and supreme importance of Conscience.

Evil of a deadened Conscience.

SECTION 3. — DUTIES TO THE WILL.

The Will is not only a most important element of our constitution, but it is the great **character-creating** The charac-force of the soul. The value of a sound, healthy, ter-creating force of the efficient Will is obvious. In order to a perfect soul. character, there must be perfect self-control, and we shall approximate perfection only as we approximate this complete command of all our powers.

Strength of Will is the great requisite for this purpose. Like other desirable qualities, this may be cul- May be culti-tivated. It is not necessary when a man has a vated. weak will, to regard it as settled that this is to be his permanent characteristic. Like every other faculty, it may be strengthened by use, or it may be weakened by disuse. If a man cultivate the habit of yielding his will to every influence that for the moment happens to be predominant, he will always be weak; that is, he will always have a weak will. If, on the contrary, he accustom himself to resist all unwholesome solicitation and impulses, even though he may do this weakly at first, this weakness will gradually change to strength; he will come, if persistent, to have command of all the forces of his being, and to direct them to whatever end seems good to him.

But it must be noticed that strength of Will by itself is not enough to constitute the ideal character. A paramount It will depend upon what is the bent of the Will, purpose. upon what is the paramount purpose. If a man makes it his chief end to advance his own interests and selfishly to pursue wealth, or fame, or power, or political preferment, and if he means to subordinate all other interests to this, he may have a powerful Will, and possess much force of character, but he will still lack immeasurably those elements which are essential to the ideal man. If, on the other hand, he has set before him, as an end to be achieved, a perfect manhood, and governs himself as he must in such a case by the principle of righteousness, suppressing whatever is at variance with this and encouraging whatever is subsidiary to it, strength of Will will not only be essential to the achievement of his purpose, but it will be enhanced by the very efforts it puts forth.

Decision, or as it is usually called, **Decision of Character,** is another constituent of a healthy Will. To be able when the facts on which a question turns are fully presented, to determine what is the proper course to pursue, and to pursue this course promptly and unhesitatingly, notwithstanding the fact, as is often the case, that there are many inducements to take the opposite course, is an invaluable trait of character. It is opposed to the vice of protracted inaction and vacillation which are the weakness of so many

Opposed to inaction and vacillation.

minds. In such cases the soul is drawn hither and thither, neither able to settle anywhere, nor having settled, to change its position ; or having settled its end, it is again moved by some real or fancied advantage in the other alternative, relenting and retreating, and perhaps sacrificing in the end all the advantages of either choice.

There are many instances in one's experience where there is no opportunity for such hesitation. The decision must be made at once, and must be final. To have trained one's self to take in the whole situation in a brief time, and to come to a quick decision, is one of the most valuable powers the soul can possess. There is, of course, a vicious side to this virtue as to most others. It consists

in determining without sufficient reflection, not regarding all the factors of the problem, and through indolence or lack of enterprise failing to ascertain all Rashness a
the elements of the case. To jump at a con- vice.
clusion, or be influenced by some prejudice, or some overbearing desire in the interest of self-indulgence, is no part of the virtue of decision.

Persistence is a characteristic of a healthy Will. Having determined on an action, or a course of conduct, after considering all the facts on which the decision properly turns, and having duly deliberated on the subject, it is generally desirable that we adhere to our purpose. Fixedness of
Fixedness of purpose is a great element of effi- purpose.
ciency. Many persons decide upon a course of action, and enter upon it with an enthusiasm that promises fruitful results; but after a certain period, when the novelty wears off, or the work becomes monotonous, or when they find unexpected obstacles, or other enterprises attract their attention, interest flags, and finally the course is abandoned. Thus they go from one project to an- Fickleness
other, and so really accomplish nothing. An and instabil-
unstable and fluctuating Will is as unfortunate ity.
as a hesitating and undecided one. The man that carefully and discriminatingly chooses and then perseveres through whatever difficulties and obstacles, is the man who not only succeeds in his vocation, but also gains the respect of his fellow-men.

This is especially the case when one decides upon an upright and virtuous life as against the oppo- Formation of
site one of self-indulgence and submission to a life-pur-
the demands of appetite and unworthy impulse. pose.
To determine on a life of rectitude after having deliber-

ately considered the whole question, and recognized the claims of Conscience and yielded to them, but subsequently to falter in presence of some strong temptation, to retreat or surrender when some vicious but attractive object presents itself, is wholly unworthy and most unmanly. It is by persistence in the face of temptation that a perpetuated righteous will or moral habit which is above all estimation comes to exist.

Like most other virtues, Persistence, carried beyond
Obstinacy is   certain limits, becomes a vice, the designation
to be avoided. of which is obstinacy, or stubbornness. When one
has made a decision as to the character of an act, or his own line of conduct, it is always possible that he may have done this on imperfect or erroneous information, or by failing to consider all the conditions. For a man to adhere to his purpose after it has been made clear to him that he is or may be wrong, is not proper persistency, but obstinacy. The thoroughly sensible man will not only guard against mistakes beforehand, but he will hold himself open to conviction, and will abandon any position he has taken when more clearly manifest truth shows that he is wrong. It is not always easy for a positive and consciously strong man to do this, but it is essential to a conscientious and well-balanced character.

Independence is a characteristic of a firm, strong, and healthy will. We must not mistake this quality for some-
A spurious   thing quite different, which often passes for
independ-   this, especially among a certain class of young
ence to be   people. The latter is a rather blatant disposi-
avoided.   tion, to be causelessly different from other people, particularly those who are older and more experienced and more thoughtful. A young man affected in this way is

pretty sure to talk largely about his "independence," and to contrast it with the "old-fogyism" of his parents and instructors and the more staid and sober members of the community. He wishes to be considered as having got beyond and above these antiquated notions, and to belong to a new order of things and as living in a more liberal atmosphere, and having a clearer understanding of what makes a great character. This, it is unnecessary to say, has nothing in common with genuine independence. It is born of self-conceit and ignorance, and is very suggestive of an empty head. But there is a real independence which is always an attribute of true nobility of character. It consists in forming one's own opinion and convictions on the evidence pre- sented, and holding them whether few others, or many or none hold them. I do not mean by this that it is defiant, or regardless of the opinion of others; but, on the con- trary, it treats these deferentially and with respect. Sometimes a person thus characterized will accept an opinion because held by others who have exceptional opportunities for knowing all the conditions and elements involved, while the person in question has none. But there are many instances where we must form our own opinions, and come to our own conclusions, each for him- self, and where those held by others constitute no reason for our own convictions. For one to adopt such views as seem to him worthy, and to maintain them whatever others may think, and at whatever cost, this is genuine and laudable independence.

Courage, Fortitude, and Patience, are virtues that one owes to one's self to cultivate. They are closely affiliated qual- ities, but differ somewhat in their signification. Most

people admire courage in a man. One who is possessed
of this quality goes out to encounter perils from which
Characteris- many would shrink. He is calm and self-pos-
tics of Cour- sessed, even when the danger is greatest, and
age. by his very calmness and steadiness of nerve
succeeds where others would fail. Courage when going
beyond its limits becomes rashness and sometimes fool-
hardiness.

We are to distinguish this quality from that boasting,
swaggering, and blustering disposition which sometimes
Modesty of goes by that name. True courage is modest,
real courage. and seldom announces itself in language, or by
any representation except in action on its proper occasions. One is struck, on reading the autobiography of
General Grant, with his depreciation of his own courage.
He almost seems to himself to be a great coward; but it
will be observed that this apparent timidity never makes
him shrink in the time of actual danger. There is no dis-
count on his courage then. Genuine courage realizes all
the perilous facts in their full force, and feels the danger
that one would avoid if it were not duty to face it. It is as
far as possible from the bravado which is not afraid because
it is not thoughtful and intelligent.

But the courage that is conspicuous on the battle-field
or in physical danger is, after all, not the highest kind.
Moral There is a **moral courage** which is nobler and
courage. more laudable, — the courage that, having con-
scientiously adopted an unpopular doctrine or policy, dares
to persist in it, though all one's friends, as well as foes,
cry out against it. Sometimes this is harder than to face
the cannon's mouth in the conflict of battle. It is the
hardest when, as sometimes with young people at school

or in other associations, one takes a position which to one's fellows, judging superficially, looks like cowardice, and when his purest motives and virtues are likely to be misapprehended, and perhaps maligned. For it is singular that courage by the weak-minded is often mistaken for pusillanimity, and the latter for the former. A young person frequently goes with the crowd, and thinks he is very brave, when, if he would reflect seriously upon his conduct, he would see that he was actuated by mere fear of public opinion, and that it was arrant cowardice that restrained him from proper action.

If courage is a disposition to encounter danger, and run the risk of great suffering, while the latter is only prospective and not yet actual, **Fortitude** exists when the suffering is present and real: it enables one to calmly endure the physical pain and the mental and moral evils to which we may be subject. In its noblest manifestation it is something more than a spirit of defiance, or than a dogged submission to what cannot be helped. It is a **What real Fortitude is.** rational acceptance of the disagreeable and distressing experience as being a part of the allotted plan of life, and capable of being utilized for some high purpose.

Patience, though nearly akin to Fortitude, is somewhat wider in its application. It implies suffering; but there are various kinds of suffering, such as petty **Difference** annoyances, the endurance of which with equa- **between Patience and** nimity we would hardly call Fortitude, but **Fortitude.** which afford a scope for Patience. Patience is also nearly synonymous with the calmness and gentleness with which certain souls bear the offensive conduct of others with whom they are placed in close relations.

These qualities of Independence, Courage, Fortitude, and Patience, taken in connection with truth, honor, honesty, and integrity, constitute what is called Manliness, — a characteristic of the grandest and loftiest kind.

Manliness.

There are also certain vices with the repression of which a firm, steady, well-educated Will has to do, such as Pride, Self-conceit, Vanity, Ambition, and a general Selfishness. Pride is inordinate Self-respect. It is frequently spoken of as within certain limits allowable and proper. Hence we have a "false pride," and other such qualifying terms to indicate a vicious kind of pride. But this seems to me not a proper use of the English language. The feeling that we have in view when Pride is spoken of as allowable is Self-respect; and this never becomes pride till it is unduly exaggerated. Pride is never a virtue.

Certain vices.

Pride always a vice.

Pride is also frequently confounded with Vanity, and is very often used when the latter is meant. Pride is estimating one's worth more highly than the conditions will justify, and exulting in this estimate. It cares little for the opinions of others. But Vanity is an overweening desire for the approval and praise of others. It is not improper to desire the approval of our fellow-men, where this desire is kept in proper subordination to other and higher impulses; but when it becomes a ruling passion, or begins to displace more worthy desires, it is not only improper, but often exceedingly offensive.

Self-conceit is a mixture of Pride and Vanity, and is apt to take on the form of Egotism, — a disposition to talk about one's self, one's exploits and capabilities. It is usually not only foolish, but also ridiculous. Selfishness is inordinate self-love. The latter is innocent, and may be a virtue: the former never is either. Difference between Self-ishness and Self-love.

Ambition, in its strict and proper signification, is an unhealthful and harmful craving for superiority. It is sometimes used in the sense of Enterprise; but as that term is sufficient for the thought which it symbolizes, there is no need of using two terms for the same conception.

PART II.

DUTIES TO OUR FELLOW-MEN.

89

DUTIES TO OUR FELLOW–MEN.

DIVISION FIRST. — JUSTICE.

Duties to our fellow-men may be grouped in two divisions, under the two heads of Justice and Beneficence.

By Justice in Ethics is signified not exactly what is meant by the same term in the administration of civil government. There it means what is in accord- Ethical and ance with the fundamental and statute laws. Civil Justice. But Justice in its full sense covers a larger field. Even a civil law may be unjust; and all such laws are to be tested by a standard higher than themselves.

Ethical Justice has reference to Rights and Obligations, — the right of others, and our own obligations to respect these rights. (Cousin says, "It is respect for the person in all that constitutes his personality." It requires us to do wrong to no one, or at least to repair the wrong already done. Its maxim is, "Do not do unto others what you do not wish they should do to you." It is what any one may have a claim upon us for, and which we are correspondingly under obligations to render.

Beneficence, on the other hand, while equally a duty on our part, may not be correspondingly claimed by others. Thus, if I have borrowed from a man a sum of money, or if he have sold me property on my promising to pay him a certain amount at a future time, he has a claim on

How Benefi-cence differs from Justice. me for so much: he may demand it of me, and has a right to it. This is the claim of Justice. If, however, he is poor and hungry, and likely to suffer, and I have the means to aid him, it is my duty to do so; but he has no right to demand this of me. I do him no positive wrong in withholding aid, though I violate my duty and am guilty of inhumanity. I transgress the law of Beneficence. Its maxim is, "Do to others as you wish to be done by."

The duties of Justice are comprised in three classes, as follows: Class I. Domestic Duties; Class II. Duties to Individuals in Society; Class III. Duties implied in organized Society, or in the relations of Government.

CLASS I. — DOMESTIC DUTIES.

CHAPTER I.

MARRIAGE.

MARRIAGE is the union of one man and one woman under mutual solemn contract to live together, and to form no other similar union "so long as they *Marriage* both shall live." It is the highest and most im- *defined.* portant of our social institutions. It is the condition and foundation of the family relations, and as such is essentially related to both human and Divine government in the world. It is, therefore, as the Ritual has it, "not by any to be entered into unadvisedly, but reverently, discreetly, and in the fear of God."

SECTION 1. — THE ETHICAL CONDITIONS OF MARRIAGE.

Not every man may properly be married to any woman. There are certain conditions which readily suggest themselves. Clearly no one should marry an idiot *Who may* or an insane person. There are certain heredi- *not marry.* tary traits that render marriage of at least doubtful propriety. No one should marry a drunkard, or a person of obviously immoral character. This is sometimes done with the expectation that the virtuous wife or husband will reform the other party. Thousands of lives have thus

93

been ruined. If a man or woman of immoral habits is not reformed before marriage, — and it should be long enough before to make it pretty sure, — there is small likelihood of reformation subsequently. There are, doubtless, exceptions, but these are scarcely so many as to more than prove the rule.

Among most civilized nations marriage is prohibited between persons within certain degrees of consanguinity. These vary somewhat in different nations; but marriage between brothers and sisters of the same family, between parents and children, between parents-in-law and children-in-law, is not sanctioned anywhere among Christian nations. It is regarded as of doubtful propriety for cousins to marry, though this rule is not strictly adhered to anywhere. In England the law prohibits a man's marrying his deceased wife's sister. In this country and in some others there is no such restriction.

It is, of course, an important ethical condition of marriage that there exist a high mutual regard, and that the Mutual regard parties be personally attractive to each other. essential. It is not necessary that there should be a passionate affection on either side. There is no doubt something meant by the expression which we find in novels, and sometimes in real life, " falling in love; " and I by no means wish to cast any contempt on the sentiment implied, which, it may be admitted, plays often an important part in the affairs of many lives. Still less would I assert that there need be no mutual love. If we are required to love all men, even our enemies, it would be monstrous to suppose that there could be real marriage where this should be wholly wanting. But that there is a necessity for that overmastering passion which we usually mean by the expression alluded to, I do not believe. It is not an essential condition of a happy conjugal union.

There is also another side to this particular subject. Where two persons have an ardent and peculiar affection for each other, that is not an absolutely conclusive reason why they should marry. There may be reasons why they should not; the situation of either party, hereditary characteristics which might render marriage unwise, physical disabilities, or tendencies, or dispositions, which may, sooner or later, result in alienation and perpetual discomfort; or there may be pre-engagements which would render such a union inconsistent with moral obligations.

Other conditions besides affection necessary.

This, at any rate, we hold to be true, that there should be a firm, steady friendship existing under conditions which promise a likelihood of permanence. To this end it is essential that each should have a positive sympathy with the other's pursuits, and be interested in the other's interests. By this is not meant that the two are to be wholly alike in character and tastes. Two persons precisely alike would be of little use to each other. The most agreeable and the most profitable association can exist only when there is difference, and difference is what constitutes individuality. Persons who have the same ideas and sentiments are very poor company for each other. Neither has anything that the other wants, and, if exclusively in each other's society, they would be no better off than if in solitude.

Friendship and sympathy.

Closely connected with these views, is the ethical objection to the union of two persons of whom one is the marked inferior of the other, intellectually or socially. There are, doubtless, cases where

Alien conditions of life.

one of the parties has had smaller advantage than the other, or belongs to a less favored grade of society. This is not a necessary bar to the conjugal contract, since there may be evident capability, as well as a disposition, for development on the part of the less fortunate party. But where there is obviously an improbability of such improvement, it would be improper to form the union.

What are sometimes called " marriages of convenience " are to be utterly deprecated on ethical grounds. When either the man or the woman, without any regard to personal fitness, and solely for the sake of wealth, or title, or rank, or other social advantage, seeks to enter the marriage state, violence is done to sacred social obligations, and the most reasonable and most serious considerations are ignored.

SECTION 2. — PERMANENCE OF MARRIAGE.

This union is clearly intended to be a permanent one. So long as both the contracting parties live, there can be innocently no dissolution. Any other supposition would logically lead to the most deplorable consequences. The moral condition of a society in which temporary unions should be formed and dissolved at the will of either party would be incalculably bad. The breaking-up of families, the sad hopelessness, especially of many women, and, worse than all, the unfortunate lot of the children of such parentage, all these render the picture one not pleasant to contemplate. Then, too, the sensual degradation and demoralization of the great mass of the population would be beyond all estimation.

It may be asked, Is there no help for persons bound by

an unfortunate marriage tie, and whose lives are thus made incalculably wretched? There are drunken husbands and besotted wives, and brutes of both sexes, to live with whom would be an undeserved punishment, even for considerable criminals, much more to worthy persons. Would it not be better that these should be divorced, and allowed each to go his or her own way? So, too, when there is an entire incompatibility of disposition, why should there be a forced companionship where the happiness of both parties would be greatly increased by separation? I do not need to dwell on the fact that, in a large proportion of instances, the evils al- Mitigation of luded to can be greatly mitigated by restraint unfortunate and mutual forbearance, and in many cases, as unions. the experience of thousands might testify, be completely done away. These evils at the worst are not as great as would ensue from making marriage an arrangement to be maintained so long as it suited the inclination of either party. But let it be admitted that there are cases in which it would be better that a separation Extreme should take place. Separation is not divorce cases. in its legal sense, nor in the sense in which that term is generally used. When so used, it implies that the parties so separated may marry again. The latitudinarian moralists who declaim eloquently and pathetically of the miseries to which men and women are condemned by reason of the indissoluble marriage bond, rarely, if ever, propose as a remedy simple separation, but such a separation or divorce as permits the forming of new unions. It would be a grand preventative of the wide prevalence of divorce in our modern communities if divorce only meant separation without the liberty of marrying again. If it be claimed

that this is a severe hardship, it will be difficult to maintain that claim in the court of sound reason.   In most of
Hardships   the relations and conditions of life, we have
not greater
than else- heavy penalties for the mistakes which we even
where in life. innocently make.   If I accidentally so injure a
limb that amputation becomes necessary, I am not to
expect that either nature or Providence will furnish me
with a new limb.   If by unwise investments I have lost
the savings of a lifetime, it will be useless for me to ask
that the economic laws shall be so readjusted that my
property will return to me.   There may be severe hardships involved in unfortunate marriages and separations
without the opportunities of a second venture; but these
hardships would be better borne by the persons who have
incurred them than that these should be remedied by a
change in our social system such as would entail untold
miseries on our communities.

SECTION 3. — POLYGAMY.

According to our definition of marriage, **Polygamy** is
excluded.   The compact must be between one man and
Monogamous one woman.   The reasons for this are not diffi-
marriages
the original   cult to find.   First, it appears to have been the
intention.   Divine intention from the beginning.   The
Bible represents to us one man and one woman as forming
the first marriage and constituting the first family.   Sec-
Other rea-   ondly, the approximate equality of the sexes
sons for re- indicates this law.   There are a few more males
garding
Polygamy as than females born; and as the former are more
wrong.   exposed than the latter to the calamities of
life, there is a substantial equality as to the number of
each sex.   Thirdly, the peace of the family is better main-

tained under this system than under that of Polygamy. There would almost inevitably be jealousies and favoritism of some, and neglect of others, not only among the wives, but among the children. Fourthly, the nations in which monogamous marriages have been maintained, have been obviously less corrupt than those in which polygamy is practised. The members of these communities are likely to be stronger physically, and to have a higher mental development. So firmly fixed is this conviction in the minds of civilized and enlightened communities, that any proposition to adopt the principle of Polygamy is regarded by detestation, even by men whose practice is not always of the purest. The local attempts to establish such a principle in certain parts of our own country are almost universally regarded as "a relic of barbarism."

SECTION 4. — RELATION OF MARRIAGE TO THE CIVIL LAW.

Marriage is not essentially an ordinance of civil society. It arises out of the constitution of humanity, and before society exists. Still, it is essential to the wel- Marriage fare of society, that civil sanctions should be prior to attached to it. Otherwise there would be no society. way of preventing abuses, and of determining the many questions that are liable to arise, because of its institution. The laws of inheritance, the rights of property Still civil of husband and wife, the regulation concerning sanction the care of children, and many other such, imply necessary. the cognizance of marriage by the government, and necessitate a definition of that which in the eye of the civil law constitutes the conjugal estate.

It is also subject to moral sanctions. Not only is it instituted by God by positive ordinance, but it is so palpably indicated in the constitution of humanity, and there are such ethical consequences connected with it, that we Moral Sanc- can scarcely doubt that it is one of the chief tion. things included in the scope of the Divine government of men. The fact that in the moral law given to the Hebrews, one of the ten great precepts prohibits adultery, and the additional fact, that in nearly all nations, polytheistic as well as monotheistic, civilized and barbarian, and even savage, the institution has a certain sacredness attached to it, and the commission of adultery is regarded not only a crime but a sin, sufficiently prove this.

CHAPTER II.

THE FAMILY.

Out of the marriage relations grow the family and the various rights and obligations pertaining thereto. Among these are comprised those of **Husband and Wife, Parents and Children, Brothers and Sisters, Masters and Servants.**

SECTION 1. — HUSBAND AND WIFE.

The duties here implied are such as inhere in the very nature of the marriage compact. Some of them are common to both, others belong to them respectively from their separate offices in the family.

First, there should be mutual fidelity. They are pledged to each other as long as both are alive. Neither has any right to form in any respect implied in the contract into which they have entered, any union or intimacy with any other person of the opposite sex. Adultery, as we have already seen, is held in reprobation and detesta- Adultery held tion by all civilized and by most uncivilized in universal nations. The moral law and the civil laws detestation. which forbid it are based on obvious principles of sound reason. We have seen what deplorable evils would result from polygamy, and from divorce at the pleasure of either party, or from the legal multiplication of the conjugal bonds on any loose pretexts. The same or worse evils would result from the promiscuous concubinage implied in a general disregard of the marriage covenant. Hence, infidelity on the part of either husband or wife is reckoned in all civilized nations, and by the precepts of the Christian religion, as sufficient reason for the severance of the conjugal tie. But it is not enough that there be no criminal act. There may not justly be any intimacy which implies a preference for the society of another over that of the lawful partner. This fidelity must be of the spirit, and not merely of the letter.

The affection or the mutual regard presumed to exist in all proper marriage, implies **kindness** and **forbearance** on both Patience and sides. There are few persons who are brought consideration. into such close and constant relationship to whom there will not come some occasions for patience and consideration. With very many it is so easy to exercise these qualities that they are scarcely noticeable. But with many it often requires some effort, and the support of moral principle. To those who subject themselves to proper moral training, the acts of self-denial and mutual sacrifice soon become lost in a sense of pleasure.

There must be a **Co-operation** on the part of both husband and wife. In the ordering of their household, in the economic measures requisite to their comfort and happiness, and in their plans for mutual culture, and the nurture of their children, they must work on some har- System and monious system. Each must contribute his or harmony. her share to the general welfare. As we have seen, in the happiest marriages it is not necessary, it is rather far from desirable, that there should be a close similarity of character, though there should be no antagonism of tastes and tendencies.

This individuality, together with that implied in the constitution of the sexes, indicates a division of labor, and that both are not to do the same things. Hence, there are certain duties that particularly devolve on the man, and certain others that specially devolve on the woman. But this individuality results in a combination as well as a division of labor, and both become contributors to the common welfare.

Individuality.

Division and Combination of labor.

This does not imply any inferiority on the part of the woman, or superiority on the part of the man. Their relation is that of co-ordination, not of subordination the one to the other. A great change has taken place in the prevailing notions as to the position of woman in the household as well as in society. As a wife she is no longer held in subjection to her husband as, theoretically at least, in even the highest ancient civilization; still less the drudge or slave, as in certain ranks of society, both in savage and, to some extent, in enlightened communities. If her perfect emancipation has not yet been achieved, as certain reformers claim, she is, at least, the companion and partner of man in all the great interests of life.

No inferiority of woman or superiority of man.

While very likely the ideal position demanded for woman by some of her zealous champions has not been attained, there is unhappily an extreme view of her proper condition, which is practically entertained by a certain class in the community. It amounts to something like this, that she is to be regarded as an ornament, a person to be labored for, and supported and ministered to, by her husband. Probably the vicious elements in the constitution of modern society have much to do with the

Not a mere ornament.

existence of this pernicious notion. It surely is not a sensible view of a wife's relation to her husband. In the ideal home, the husband no more supports the wife than the wife supports the husband; but they both labor together, and conspire to build up each other's fortune and happiness and character.

> " . . . in the long years liker must they grow;
> The man be more of woman, she of man;
> He gain in sweetness and in moral height,
> Nor lose the wrestling thews that throw the world;
> She mental breadth, nor fail in childward care,
> Nor lose the childlike in the larger mind;
> Till at last she set herself to man,
> Like perfect music unto noble words;
> And so these twain, upon the skirts of Time,
> Sit side by side, full-summ'd in all their power,
> Dispensing harvest, sowing the To-be,
> Self-reverent each and reverencing each,
> Distinct in individualities,
> But like each other ev'n as those who love.
> Then comes the statelier Eden back to men:
> Then reign the world's great bridals, chaste and calm:
> Then springs the crowning race of human kind.
> May these things be!"

SECTION 2. — RIGHTS AND OBLIGATIONS OF PARENTS.

The parent has a right to order the child's life in most respects, especially during all its early years. This arises from the fact of responsibility for the training of the child, and from the very nature of the family as a place for such training. Hence the parent has a right to the

Not a permanently absolute right.

respect, affection, and obedience of the child, both for the sake of order in the household and for the child's own physical and moral health. That this right is not permanently absolute is evident.

The very training of the child involves the expectation of its own self-government and responsibility; therefore, in proportion as these increase, the authority of the parent diminishes, till, at a certain time which it is impossible to accurately fix, it ceases altogether.

The parent has a right to the earnings of a child in all these cases where, within the limits of certain years, there are any earnings. This limit it might not be possible to define accurately; but, for the sake of preventing dispute and wrangling, society fixes the time at twenty-one years of age.

The parent has no right to maltreat the child, or to do anything to render it physically or mentally incapable, or to compel any immoral conduct or habit. In- Limitation of dustrial training, on the contrary, so far as the the parental circumstances will allow, is a duty. The right. child is to be furnished the means of Education, and to be trained to good habits of moral conduct, and pre- pared for the position of a good and useful member of society.

SECTION 3. — RIGHTS AND OBLIGATIONS OF CHILDREN.

Children, as well as parents, have **Rights.** These, like their **Obligations,** are partly indicated in the corresponding obligations and rights of parents.

First, the child has a right to **Life** and all that is implied in its support, so far as it is in the power of the parent to supply it. The very fact that the parent has Rights of caused the child to be, confers upon the latter children. this right, and upon the parent the corresponding obliga- tion. Furthermore, it is the right of the child that his existence should not be made so miserable that it would be better not to be. There are multitudes of children whose miseries seem to almost reach this sad level. In many cases it is the misfortune rather than the fault of the parents; but in many others it comes from either needless negligence, or because of conditions for which the parents are criminally responsible. The child, as has been implied, has a right to suitable industrial training, and to such education and moral instruction as will fit him to make his way in the world, and become a useful member of society.

The child's duty is, first of all, to **Obey his parents.** This, when he first begins to perceive the relations between **Duties of** himself and them, is supreme and absolute. **children.** Subsequently there will be higher duties; but these will be learned only through the former. With increasing years, and the development of his personality, this obligation of the child becomes modified, and at last may cease altogether.

The child is also under obligation to show **Respect** and **Kindness** to parents. Natural affection would impel this; and it is a laudable condition of the child's mind, in which these are the result of spontaneous impulse instead of enforced as duties. A child in whom they are wanting is rightly regarded by members of the community not only as unworthy but unnatural, and in a sense abhorrent. These sentiments do not, like the duty of obedience, diminish with increasing years, but rather grow with the growth. Even if the parent should become immoral and unworthy, it is still the duty of the child to show him respect and kindness, simply because he is his parent.

SECTION 4. — DUTIES OF BROTHERS AND SISTERS.

The family is a little commonwealth by itself. It is here that the members are trained for membership in the larger communities of their fellow-men, and for the duties and responsibilities of human society. The family a community. Hence the obligations existing are, in a more simple and rudimentary form, the obligations which exist between men in the world at large. The general end to be sought is the peace and harmony of the household, and the happiness and healthful development of all its members.

Kindness and **Affection** stand foremost here as in other family relations. Nature will inspire these to a certain extent, unless it is thwarted and perverted. Duties implied. Whenever this is unhappily the case, there are means of restoring the proper spirit. Reasonable consideration of the relation existing, and of the evil implied in wrong and malevolent dispositions, and of the happiness which would result both to the individual and to the family from kindly conduct, would ordinarily produce a sensible state of feeling. Few things are more deplorable than domestic dissensions, the selfishness of individual members of the family, jealousies, rivalries, perpetual strifes, and bickering.

To prevent these, there must be **mutual forbearance.** There will always be something in the conduct of each which may produce more or less annoyance to others. There will be opportunities for the exercise of patience and the overlooking of many faults and errors. Each may well remember that he is himself imperfect.

There should be **mutual helpfulness.** No one is quite

sufficient unto himself anywhere in this world. This great lesson must be learned first of all in the domestic community. Every one has something that another has not; each lacks something needful for his welfare which another has. Much of this is of a kind that imparting does not diminish; and even where sacrifice is implied, that becomes a valuable element in the building of character. It is especially the duty of the elder to help the younger, while the latter in a hundred ways may reciprocate the kindness of the former.

There should be **equality** among the children. Not that they are to be all alike. This they are not by their

Equality does not imply similarity of character.

natural constitutions, and it is not required that this should be sought by culture. It is better that there should be variety than sameness; but there is a certain equality of right. No one can properly assume superiority in this respect because of age, or of physical strength or comeliness, or as having more brilliant mental parts than another. If superior gifts exist in any one, instead of making them the occasion of higher privilege or of exemption from duty, they should rather be thankfully used as a means of aiding others less favored. Greater powers imply greater obligations and more numerous duties.

SECTION 5. — MASTERS AND SERVANTS.

In many families servants constitute a part of the household. We are not to shrink from the thought that they

Servants as members of the family.

are members of the family. I mean, of course, such servants as are permanently domesticated, and live under the same roof with other members of the family. This is an important relation, and implies mutual rights and corresponding duties. In the first place, a servant in our own country and in many others is not a slave but a free person; and his rights are those of a freeman. Ordinarily they are under contract voluntarily entered into, to render service of a specified kind and under certain stipulated conditions. A part of the conditions in the kind of service we are now considering is, that they are to have a home in the house of their employer. Hence they are to be treated not as though they belonged to another and inferior To be treated class, but as possessing all the rights of human not as be-longing to an beings. I do not now discuss the duty of pay- inferior class. ing them fairly for their work, and observing all the conditions of the contract, as these will be considered under another head; but their opinions and convictions, and even their prejudices, so long as they do not interfere with their duties, and do not lead to practical immorality, are to be respected. This embraces both their religious opinions and their political views. Furthermore, it is the duty of all employers to make their employees as happy as circumstances will admit.

On the other hand, it is the duty of servants to show all fidelity to those who employ them. This they may do without loss of manliness or womanliness, and without lapsing into a degrading servility. There is no Duties of reason why employees in any situation should Servants. not have a sensible independence. But care should be taken that this does not assume an offensive form, as springing out of conceit, or as being the outcome of a contentious spirit.

CLASS II.—DUTIES TO INDIVIDUALS IN SOCIETY.

HERE again we find that all men have rights as well as obligations; also, that where a right exists a corresponding obligation exists somewhere else. Among these rights which are to be respected, both by society and by individuals, are: 1. Life; 2. Liberty; 3. Property; 4. Character; 5. Reputation; 6. Veracity. Justice demands of us that we do not intentionally violate any of these rights.

Various kinds of rights.

CHAPTER I.

LIFE.

SECTION 1. — THE SACREDNESS OF LIFE.

GENERALLY speaking, every man has a right to Life who has not forfeited that right by some crime. Our first duty, then, is not to interfere with this right. We may not commit murder.

Looked at from a natural point of view, and with reference to this world, it is the greatest wrong we can inflict upon a man. It is true, that there are evils that a

110

man would rather lose his life than endure. Men have freely given up their lives when the alternative was the denial of their religious faith, or subjecting themselves to some dishonor, or that they might save those whom they love. For the sake of their country, or because of some other great interest they have had at heart, they have put their lives in peril. But this generally has been their own offering. Except in the last case mentioned, no one has a right to subject them to this sacrifice. The nation has the right to put its citizens in peril for its own salvation and in its own defence. *The greatest wrong possible.*

Voluntary surrender of life for a worthy purpose.

It is also true, that a man may forfeit his life by crime. I do not undertake to discuss the question of capital punishment. There are certainly very strong arguments for its entire abolition. There are also cogent arguments in favor of it. I am disposed to believe that in our present state of civilization and in civilized nations, it may safely be dispensed with. In some of our own state governments the experiment has been tried; and although there are those who think they discern an increase of crime because of the change, others, equally candid, discern no change for the worse. Certainly the results are not so obvious as to prove conclusive against the abolition. *Forfeiture of the right to life by crime.*

But in any case, the death penalty for certain crimes is in the judgment of most nations considered necessary to the protection of society. Whether this is a wise judgment may be doubted; but even if untrue, the infliction of the penalty is not a violation of the right of the criminal to life. By his crime he has forfeited his life, whether it be the better policy for the community to exact it or not. Still, in all cases he has a right to the most thorough investigation, and to whatever vindication may be possible, and he should not be condemned except on indisputable evidence.

SECTION 2. — WAR.

It is an important question whether the taking of life in war is justifiable. The main question here is whether *Is War ever justifiable?* war itself is ever justifiable; for if war exists, then the taking up of arms and the slaughter of foes are inevitable. The ostensible object of an army is to destroy the lives of those composing an opposing army. It would, no doubt, be one of the altogether best things for humanity if war were entirely abolished. The associations of men and women who seek this end are engaged in the noblest of undertakings. There is no question that there are better methods for settling national disputes. But neither this nor the fact that there is never a war which did not involve some selfishness and wrong on the part of one party or the other, if not of both, proves that war is never justifiable. Wars cannot entirely cease except by the unanimous consent of nations; and for one nation to declare that it would in no case engage in war, not even to resist invasion, might render it an easy prey to the greed and selfishness of others. So, too, it may be the case that a nation does all in its power to avert a war; but an antagonist may declare war against it, and invade its territory. In such a case it seems evident that self-defence is its duty at whatever cost. So that we cannot say that war may not sometimes be justifiable.

Then, again, the very existence of government implies power to execute its laws, and this involves the possibility of using force. Evil-doers must be coerced, violence must sometimes be suppressed by violence. The whole police system is in some sense a system of war, The police or at least implies a possibility of war. Riots plies possible and insurrections, and combinations of all war. sorts against the execution of the laws, must be put down, or there is an end to civil government, and an inauguration of anarchy.

Unquestionably the great majority of wars might be prevented were either party in real earnest to maintain peace. The majority of wars, we might perhaps say all wars, arise from some immoral action or pur-War involves pose on the part of one or more of the nations wrong some-engaged in them. They are so far forth un-where. justifiable, not only in the fact that they destroy human life, but that they do other vast and irreparable injury.

If the nations would agree upon the practicable scheme of an **international tribunal** before which all differences should be brought, and where decisions should International be final, wars would cease at once. That this arbitration. is practicable is evident not only from the fact that most serious disputes have been decided by arbitration, but from the fact that this is substantially the method of determining the difference between the local governments of great nations. Notably is this the case with the states of our own Federal Union. No one of the individual states thinks of going to war with another. There has never been an instance of hostile collision, so far as I recollect. If a conflict arises, there are peaceable and rational ways of settling it. It is true, there has been a great civil war, but this was not so much of states as of sections. What is possible and practicable between

RUDIMENTARY ETHICS.

such states as ours, is possible and practicable between nations. A Congress of nations could easily reconcile all differences of opinion and all conflicting claims. This would save all the wanton destruction of human life involved in war: it would also prevent the vast destruction of property and other incalculable losses, many of which are the occasions of wide-spread misery in communities, and which tend to shorten multitudes of human lives.

SECTION 3. — TRADES WHICH WORK MISCHIEF IN THE COMMUNITY.

It is a violation of this right to engage in any business the effect of which is to endanger human life, or to bring it to an earlier close than would otherwise take place. There are several employments of this kind. The most prominent and most destructive is, of course, the Liquor traffic. It is said by those who would defend this business, that no one is forced to indulge in the use of alcoholic beverages; that it is wholly voluntary, and that Sophistical it is not necessary to suppose that all those arguments in favor of an who partake of such beverages do endanger evil practice. actually their lives or the lives of those dependent upon them. Conceding this for the sake of the argument, it still remains that probably nine-tenths, and possibly nineteen-twentieths, of these dealers in such commodities would have no basis for their business, and no inducement to remain in it, but for the patronage of those who are perilling their lives and the lives of those dependent upon them by their indulgence. The command "Thou shalt not kill," runs, if not as directly, yet as surely, against this class of life-destroying agents as against those who, with knife or pistol or bludgeon, threaten the lives of their fellow-men. When one man puts a pistol to the head of another, and demands his money or his life, he does not compel him absolutely to give up his money, but he puts him in a position where he is pretty sure to do it. So the powerful temptations which are spread in the sight of a man given to appetite do not compel him to get drunk, yet they put him in a condition where he is morally certain to do so.

I have mentioned only one kind of occupation as being murderous in its character. There are others that are less obviously and less extensively, but not less actually so. Every kind of article produced by the skill or labor of man the main, I do not say the sole, use of *All kinds of* which results in the diminution of human life, *business the* and every business the object of which is to *product of which tend* increase the facilities for the indulgence of *to diminish* unwholesome appetites, or for physically harm- *tion of this* ful practices, come under this head. Such in- *right.* dulgence and such practices not only are evil in the first instances, but they tend to fasten a habit on the subject of them which is enslaving and degrading; and what is still worse, the habit is sometimes transmitted to children. Very often diseases and weakness thus generated and which diminish life become hereditary, and this bad inheritance does not always terminate with the second generation.

SECTION 4. — HATRED AND UNKINDNESS.

It may seem to some as going to an extreme to say that **Hatred of our fellow-men** tends to the violation of the right of life. But we have the authoritative assertion of a superhuman wisdom that "he that hateth his brother in his heart is a murderer." This statement is certainly not altogether irrational, even if the utterance were not

The nature of Hatred and its possible extremes. clothed with authority. For what is the nature of Hatred? Is it not essentially to wish ill to its object? How great that ill may be depends upon the intensity of the passion. As the worst ill that can be desired for any one is death, it needs only a certain degree of hatred to inspire that desire, and such desire in multitudes of instances only waits an opportunity to secure its gratification. No one knows when he begins to cherish hatred towards another to what lengths it may carry him, or in what crime it may end. The only safety is to stifle such a passion in its conception.

There are other ways in which the lives of men are shortened through the agency of their fellows. **Maltreatment** of children or servants by overwork, or by want of

Life shortened by needless exposure. those things essential to health, or by unnecessary exposure of various kinds, often puts their lives in peril. On the other hand, indulgences on the part of parents have similar results, as when palatable but improper food, fashionable but unhealthy styles of dress, irregular habits, nocturnal excitements and consequent exposure, are permitted or encouraged. No doubt thousands every year fall victims to such usages.

SECTION 5. — DUELLING.

It may seem nugatory to speak here of the **Duel** as a violation of the sacredness of human life. Happily it has now come to be almost universally reprobated in all civilized communities; and although it long persisted in practice, even after it was theoretically discarded, it is now become nearly obsolete, and needs little argument to convince us of its detestable character. It seems scarcely

credible that men brought up in highly civilized Christian
communities should have for so many ages cherished this
barbarous custom : that because of a fancied or   <small>Absurdity of</small>
even a real insult, men should challenge one <small>the custom.</small>
another to a murderous contest in which one or the other,
and perhaps both, were likely to lose their lives. It was
both wicked and senseless. Men were considered brave
who did this, and to avoid such a contest was regarded as
cowardly. The rules by which it was justified and regulated were called the "Code of honor," and the character
of the transaction was reckoned as chivalrous in the highest degree. Yet to sober and sensible minds it appears
rather like lack of courage which led men to engage in
such encounters. It might better be regarded as fool-
hardy than chivalrous, and that which regulated it
appears more like a code of dishonor than of honor.
Why it should be considered as settling anything, or heal-
ing any mental hurt, or rescuing an imperilled reputation,
when one man has insulted another, either to kill the
other, or to run the risk of being killed by him, is not
at all obvious. That a man of hot temper, under strong
provocation, and in great excitement, should assault and
kill his opponent, wicked as it is, admits at least of some
mitigation ; but when two men proceed deliberately, and
with ample time, to make all their preparations, and
therefore for reason and good judgment to resume their
sway, there is no room for palliation, and such conduct
deserves contempt as well as condemnation.

SECTION 6. — SELF-DEFENCE.

It is not intended in anything that has been said in the
foregoing sections to deny the right of individual self-

defence. We have already inferred the justification of national self-protection, even to the extent of war and the consequence of the destruction of life as against those assaulting the nation. This is not the less obvious in the case of the individual. Possibly the right of the former **Self-defence** is developed from that of the latter. This **instinctive and sponta-** seems to be among the instincts of every **neous.** human being. There is a spontaneous impulse, when we are assaulted, to use every means to preserve ourselves from death or injury. This defence may go to the very extent necessary for this purpose, even to **Limitations** sacrificing the life of the assaulter. But we **of this right.** have no right to go further than what is thus essential to self-protection. We may not take his life unless there be a probability that it is the only way of preserving our own. No injustice is done him in this case, since by his attempt to destroy another life, he has forfeited his own.

It would not be just, when once we have been freed from danger, to pursue our foe vindictively. To kill him, or to do him any bodily harm, when it is evident that his hostility cannot be the cause of any injury, would be a violation of moral obligation and might be murder.

This principle will bear extension to the defence of **Defence of** those who are dependent upon us. Should the **one's family.** father of a family find a villain attempting to murder his wife and children, if there were no other obvious way to prevent this crime, he would be justified in taking the life of the invader, and it would not be wise to deliberate very long as to the probabilities of other means of prevention.

CHAPTER II.

LIBERTY.

NEXT to one's life, the most highly prized boon of a human being is Liberty. By Liberty we mean the unobstructed use of one's powers in any way that may seem good to him. A child might describe it as doing and having whatever one wants to do or have, and having and doing nothing that he does not want to do or have. This is the perfect ideal liberty, and as such it could probably not be more happily set forth. Yet evidently this ideal liberty is seldom, and perhaps never, actualized among men; and it is approximated only through much and careful moral training. Until this training is complete, our liberty has its limitations. Since every man has this right in common with every other man, the right of each becomes the limit of that of his fellows. I may want my neighbor's horse; but he wants it too, and as we cannot both have it, one must do without it. That the right to the horse is his and not mine, is clear from the fact that he is the possessor of it, unless it can be shown that he has violated some right of mine in getting possession of it. My liberty, then, consists in the privilege of doing and having whatever it is in my power to do and have, provided that I do not exercise this power in violation of the right of any other person.

Definition and illustration. Ideal Liberty.

Limitations of Liberty.

SECTION 1. — LIBERTY UNDER LAW.

It has been shown, in a previous part of this book, that the motive and impulses of a man conflict with one another, so that even subjectively, with most men, real liberty does not exist. It must be achieved by the education and discipline of the desires. They must be brought into harmony with one another by being made severally to harmonize with the one great paramount principle of the Divine Law.

It is a crude and superficial yet somewhat popular notion, Liberty not antagonistic to Law, but the contrary. that Liberty and Law are antagonistic. This is utterly untrue. LIBERTY UNDER LAW is the only real and complete Liberty in the Universe. We might illustrate this truth by reference to the condition of our communities, as they are more or less under a system of civil law. Where do we find the largest Liberty? Is it in those communities where laws are few, imperfect, inadequate, and only partially executed; or in those in which there is a thorough system of laws, calculated to reach and guard the rights of all citizens, and where they are thoroughly executed? The question answers itself to every mind. In the communities where most of us live, the laws are numerous and effective, and they are carefully executed. But is any upright citizen burdened by the pressure of these laws? Men go about their daily business, and from morning to night, and from the beginning of the week to its end, they are unconscious of the restrictions laid upon them, and they seldom think of the laws except as some one wantonly violates them. They have been accustomed to subject themselves to this condition all their lives, and it has become a kind of second nature to them.

What is true of the civil law is true also, only in a far greater degree, of the moral law; since the moral law is perfect, while the civil law at best falls short of perfection by a considerable interval. As we have seen, men here in this world are under the influence of conflicting desires; and it is this conflict that causes a very large part of the unhappiness of the race. Such a state is also incompatible with genuine liberty. Over all there is the moral law with its retribution and its rewards. It is of supreme authority, and hence all impulses and desires are to be subject to it. The great business of every man is to bring himself into harmony with this. It is the only means *The largest liberty conditioned on the subjection of all desires to the supreme moral law.* by which this painful restriction will cease and genuine liberty can exist. Until these inferior cravings are subjected, the law will press unequally on the soul. If a man were to lie upon a hard rock, even if the surface were smooth, the whole weight of the body would be supported at a few points, and would be very painful. If, by any means, the rock could be chiselled out so as to conform to the exact shape of the body, there would be no more discomfort than in lying upon a bed of down, because every part of the body would be equally supported; or, in other words, the support would press equally upon every part. This may be illustrated again by the pressure of water upon a fish, or of the air upon our bodies. It is said that the pressure of the atmosphere upon the body is equal to that of many tons. If it were not even and uniform it would cause intense suffering, as indeed it sometimes does when, by fortuity, any portion of the body is exposed to

an undue pressure. Analogous to this is the relation of
the human spirit to the moral law. It must be adjusted
Our charac- to it so that there will be no painful pressure
ter to be ad- at any point. This adjustment is the end of
justed to uni-
versal law. moral culture ; and the closer the approxima-
tion to perfection this is, the larger the liberty of the
soul.

In such a state the desires will be properly regulated
and subordinated. The inferior will at once yield to the
superior, and all to the supreme law. Men will do what
they ought to do, not because they must, but because they
want to do so. They will have and do what they desire,
and nothing that they do not desire, simply because they
desire what is right and nothing else. This is what is
meant by "Liberty under Law." In no world, nor in any part
of the universe, in time nor in eternity, can we conceive
of any other perfect liberty. Whatever may be our conception of heaven, it will be false if we regard it as a
place or state in which there is no law. Law the most
thorough and all-pervading exists there; but it reveals
itself by no effect of restraint or constraint on its subjects, since it presses so equally and uniformly on every
individual and the whole society, that no one is conscious
of its presence, any more than men or animals are conscious of the atmosphere in which they live. It produces
no antagonism and interferes with no one's liberty.

SECTION 2. — LIBERTY IN OUR SOCIAL RELATIONS.

I have dwelt so long on subjective individual liberty as
containing the germ of the whole doctrine of liberty in all
possible human relations. The moral law, as we have
seen, is no restriction upon the liberty of moral beings,

but rather the promoter of it. Yet it demands that we sacredly respect the liberty of our fellow-men. This does not imply, as has been seen, that society is to Our desires allow men to do whatever they may desire to do limited by the desires of if in so doing they interfere with the rights of our fellow- others. If one desires to have my farm, or my men. horse, or my books, and attempts to gratify that desire against my consent, he is met, by both civil and moral law, with the stern utterance, "Thou shalt not;" and the whole force of society may be summoned to restrain his action. It is not liberty in defiance of law to which he has a right, but *liberty under law.* Men may forfeit their liberty, as well as their lives, by crime, and may be deprived of it by imprisonment or by other restrictions. There are many ways in which men are unjustly Ways in deprived of their liberty. It has been shown which the that every man has a right to himself, — that is, liberty is to all the powers of body and mind which he violated. possesses, to use them in any way that seems good to him, provided that he does not interfere with the rights of any other man, or violate the requirements of the moral law.

First, a man has a right to his physical powers and to use them as he pleases. He may go anywhere at his own option, provided such action does not trench upon another's rights, or upon the rights of society. He may engage in any occupation which will not endanger the life or property or other interest of any one else. He may work or be idle; and, so far as other men are concerned, it is no business of theirs, unless by so doing he transgresses the aforesaid limits. He may eat and drink according to his own inclinations, and dress as he chooses, subject to the same conditions.

This right is violated when a man is **compelled to remain in one locality,** or at least to make his home there, as has

Locomotion
and occu-
pation.

sometimes been required in certain European communities, lest he should become a burden to another parish than that in which he has been brought up. It is also violated when he is compelled to learn a particular trade against his own preference, as, for instance, the trade of his father. But he may not pursue an occupation that is dangerous to the community, as if one should enter upon the manufacture of gunpowder in the immediate vicinity of dwelling-houses. If, however, he has established his business at a safe distance from human habitations, and after it is established others see fit to build in the vicinity, they do it at their own risk : he has a right to continue his business. So of a slaughter-house or other such offensive enterprise.

It may be said that he may make an unwise choice, and thereby effect his injury. That is his own affair, and he

That he use
his liberty
improperly
no reason for
depriving a
man of it.

must bear the consequences. It may also be said that, if left to his own preference, he may choose to spend his time in idleness, and that this would be a great wrong in itself, and might likewise result in starvation, or make him a burden to the community. It would no doubt be a great wrong, but it is one that he must settle with God and not with his fellow-men. As to his becoming a burden on the community, that is optional with the community. It is under no obligation to support a man who is in danger of starving through indolence. If left to receive the natural penalty of his idleness, it would be likely to operate as a warning to others. While there no doubt are instances where it would be better for the individual if he were compelled to labor, and to do this in some particular occupation rather than another, still the loss to men in general by relieving them of their responsibility and depriving them of their power of self-disposal, would be incalculably greater than the gain in exceptional instances. It is subtracting greatly from a man's value, and is an unjust reduction of his manhood, to allow any other choice than his own in these matters to which we have referred.

There are doubtless some apparent exceptions to the application of these general principles. Most prominent among these is, that society has a right to regu- Exceptions to late the employment of married women in the applica- factories. It may do this on the assumption principles. warrantable, as it seems to me, that a woman may be so employed as to neglect her children, and therefore be acting in violation of their rights. Under this view of it there is not even an exceptional violation of the principle. So, too, I do not see that it is inconsistent with the same principle to compel a lazy, shiftless man who has a family, to work and do something for their support.

SECTION 3. — SLAVERY.

To deprive a man of all these rights, or to put him in respect of them at the disposal of another man, is slavery. Happily there is at this day no great need of elaborate discussion of this subject, since in our communities and in our nation, as well as in most civilized nations, this evil system has been done away. It is amazing that such a system could have existed so long in a Christian nation; astonishing too are the arguments which were offered in its defence. That one man should own another, and deprive him of all power of managing his own person, of acquiring and possessing property, and of all domestic privileges, seems to us here and now almost monstrous.

Happily, after the agonizing struggle of ages, the question has been settled in favor of individual liberty. Theoretically, at least, it is almost universally admitted that every man owns himself, and no one is any longer a chattel personal or subject to the control of another. Still there are instances of oppression in nearly all our communities, where, by the advantage of position or power, the strong virtually subject the weak to their dictation, and practically deprive them of their freedom. It is true this is not universal or general, nor where it occurs is it often absolute; but there are many instances in which poor men unfavorably situated are made to do and suffer what they would not but for the fear of having their lives made still more wretched by the rapacity and selfishness of those who have the advantage over them. Employers do not always have it in their power to oppress or deal unfairly with those who labor for them; and many who have the power do not exercise it after a selfish fashion. But there are many instances in which this power is exercised, and the effects are seen in the hopeless poverty of not only laborers but of those dependent on them. This evil is being considered and investigated by good men and women, and measures are more and more being put in operation to remedy these abuses. The growing intelligence and capability of the great masses of laboring men are also promising in this respect.

Still instances of virtual slavery.

SECTION 4. — MENTAL LIBERTY.

Man has a right to the control and ownership not only of his physical powers but also of his **mental and moral faculties.** Corresponding to this right on the one part is the obligation on the other. A man, then, has a right to use his mind as he chooses under the limita- What is im-tions elsewhere obtaining that he do not inter- plied in men-fere with the rights of others. He may **read** tal liberty. **what he pleases,** and **pursue any studies** for which he has an inclination, and pursue them as far as he pleases. If he has reached the age of maturity and self-government, and has never yet learned to read, he may do so now or he may remain in ignorance as he chooses.

If it be said that in so doing certain men might study what is unprofitable and harmful, or might read vicious books or those which inculcate false doctrines, Objections this is all true; and no doubt it would be that a man better in some instances for certain persons if might use this liberty they were restrained. But for the vast majority to his own it is better that they take the responsibility of harm and the governing themselves; and if they make mis- community. takes or follow evil inclinations in this respect or in others, the consequences are their own. To interfere would be productive possibly of a little good, but of so very much more evil that it would better be avoided. No men and no set of men are wise enough to determine what any other man should read or study, any more than what he should eat or drink or wear; and to give this right to any persons or to society would be so far to curtail the liberty of the individual. So too every man has a right to **publish his thoughts** to the world, and to do this

orally or by writing. He must do it under the same
limitations as have been set down elsewhere.
He may not come into an assembly of people
gathered for a purpose of their own, and insist
on discussing a subject that interests no one but himself,
or that those who are present do not generally care to
hear about. Nor may he come into my family, and ven-
tilate doctrines that I do not wish to have presented there
except by myself or some one whom I might choose and
trust to do this. Nor may he properly, without my consent, come into my factory or workshop or school-room,
and proceed to present his thoughts, and divert those who
are present from the proper business of the occasion. But
in any private company assembled for the purpose of
hearing him, or who consent to his speaking, or in any
place of public assembly to which he has invited the public that he may address them, or in any newspaper or
other periodical to which he may have access, or in any
pamphlet or book which he may publish, he may freely
set forth his views, provided that, in so doing, he does not
interfere with the rights of others. If these views are
wrong, let them be refuted with the same freedom as they
are set forth. No one may say that I am wrong and he
is right; but he has the privilege of proving this if he can.

But a man may set forth not only notions that are false,
but those which, if carried out, are bad and injurious.
Should he not be restrained? Not unless the publication
tends directly and obviously to incite men to disorderly
and unlawful conduct. As long as it is a mere matter
of opinion or theory, no matter how erroneous it is, the
liberty of the writer should not be infringed. The reason
of this is fairly obvious. Every false doctrine is, no doubt,

Rights of promulga-tion.

harmful to some extent. But then most opinions, though believed by some, are pretty certain to be regarded as false by others. Hence were we at liberty to prevent the publication of opinions deemed false by any, very few publications would be permitted, and freedom of thought and utterance would cease, — a policy upon which only the most despotic governments would now venture. The only safe remedy of a free people against *Should not be restricted, even if his views are pernicious, as long as it is mere matter of opinion.* the utterance of pernicious sentiments by tongue or pen, is the exposure of their evil character by the same instrumentalities, and thus give the public an opportunity to judge concerning the views presented.

To this limit, but not much further, may intellectual liberty proceed. So long as men only *promulgate* and *advocate* pernicious theories and policies, they may be tolerated. But when they begin to urge others to put them in practice, and excite them to unlawful acts, then liberty changes to license, and they *Not at liberty to incite others to unlawful acts.* become obnoxious to public law and public order. A man may teach that property is robbery, and that what one has accumulated another may innocently take for his own use. This may be refuted by wise and sensible reasoners, and no great harm be done. But if, in addition to this, it be advised and urged upon the thoughtless to steal and plunder, the adviser may properly be restrained by the government, and made to suffer the penalty of such criminal conduct.

So also if a man publish any such opinion as tends to injure the reputation of another, he transgresses the proper limit of freedom of utterance. He is violating the right of his fellows, and no one can justly do this under the

cover of intellectual liberty.   The freest governments prohibit such utterances, or at least make those who indulge

**Nor at lib-
erty to vio-
late the right
to reputa-
tion.**
themselves in them liable to suffer a proper
penalty.   Still, so jealous are we under such a
government as ours of any restriction of the
liberty of the press, that our journals are
allowed to go to, if not beyond, the very verge of mis-
chievous and disgraceful license.   In a political campaign

**Mischief of
license in
this respect.**
the abuse lavished upon a candidate for office
of the opposite party is appalling.   The only
redeeming feature in such a case is that the
extravagance of defamation is so great that few really
believe what is published; not unfrequently it is dismissed
both by the friends of the person assailed and by the public generally as a "campaign lie."   In this respect men
may and do in innumerable instances avoid amenability to
the civil law, while flagrantly violating the most important ethical obligations.   Certainly there is little danger
among us of erring on the side of too great restriction of
the freedom of the press and of public speech, but much
of going to the opposite extreme.

SECTION 5. — RELIGIOUS LIBERTY.

Religious Liberty implies the right of every person to
entertain and profess such religious convictions and doctrines as seem to him most reasonable, and to put in prac-

**In what it
consists.**
tice the principles implied, under the familiar
limitations.   He may have any religion he
chooses ; or, if he so choose, he may reject all religions,
being accountable to none but his Maker.   He may adopt
such ceremonies or ritual as seems to him desirable, and
attend any assemblies or unite with any ecclesiastical

body whose views and regulations are adapted to meet his religious wants. This right is violated when men are required to worship God in any particular way; when they are forbidden to worship in some particular form; when they are forbidden to worship in any way at all; or when they are subjected to disabilities, political or otherwise, because of their profession or non-profession of a particular faith. These disabilities may be imposed by the government or by public sentiment. Men and women are sometimes socially ostracized because they belong to a certain religious party or sect. All such treatment is a violation of right, and is therefore immoral and unjust.

But religious liberty, like intellectual, may pass beyond its legitimate bounds, and become the pretext for conduct detrimental to personal rights and to the. interests of society. No pretence of religious devotion or usage can justify conduct of any sort which is harmful to the prosperity or the morals of the community. Suppose a religious denomination adopts the theory of Polygamy, as the Mormons, or the Oneida community of several years ago, and not only adopts the theory, but proceeds to apply it in practice. If polygamy is regarded by the nation as a practice that is incalculably harmful and every way detestable, it makes no difference whether it is attempted under the guise of religion or in some other way, it must be put down by society in its own defence. The suppression of it by law can no more be regarded as religious persecution than the suppression of a gang of men associating themselves for the purpose of robbery, and proceeding to carry out their purposes, but accompanying their performance by certain religious rites, would be considered persecution. Their depredations may not be allowed any more because they had blasphemously undertaken to throw over them the sanction of religion than if they were to put their schemes in execution by the ordinary methods.

CHAPTER III.

PROPERTY.

SECTION 1. — THE RIGHT OF PROPERTY.

The right of property arises out of the general right of a man to himself, — that is, his right to all his powers of body and mind, to use them in his own way. From this it follows that any effect that he can cause in Genesis of this use of them belongs to him. If by any the right of labor upon any material which nature has fur- property. nished me, without the aid of any one else, I have produced something of value, that is mine. Any utility which I have made available I have a right to appropriate and enjoy, and no other person has any right to it or any part of it. If I live near the sea, and go out on it and catch fish, the fish are mine. If I go in the forest and secure wild game for food, the game is mine. If, out of timber and lumber and other material which have come into my possession, I construct a house on land belonging to me, the house is my property. The ownership in all these cases is exclusive, except, as may be shown hereafter, the civil government under which I live, and which secures to me my personal rights of all kinds, has a claim upon it for my share of the cost of the maintenance of the system.

In the cases supposed, the ownership is absolute except

as indicated. There are other cases in which it is partial and limited. If I raise crops on land in possession of an-other man, then only a part of the product is mine. If out of material furnished by another, I construct implements or furniture, these are partly his, until I render him some equivalent. So in all the relations of wages and capital, a part only of the product belongs to the laborer, and for that he usually receives what is supposed to be an equivalent in money or some commodity.

Partial and limited own-ership.

Furthermore, in the relation of employer and employee, the former, by virtue of his ability to manage the busi-ness so as to make it as productive as possible, may prop-erly claim a share of the product, usually a larger share than the latter; because it is by his skill and ability that it becomes so great as it is. If such power and ability were not exerted, the results of labor, even to the manual laborer, might be only a small fraction of what it now is. The employer in the sense of the manager of the business, and not necessarily as a capitalist which he frequently is not, is a productive laborer, and as such is as truly as any other laborer entitled to that proportion of the whole product of which he is the efficient cause. A part of the difficulty between employers and laborers occurs at this point. Demagogues and inconsiderate zealots often teach that all property is created by labor, meaning muscular or manual labor; whereas only a small fraction of it is so created; though it is true that, in a very important sense, all property is created by labor. But in this case we must include mental as well as manual labor; for more of the wealth of the world is due to this kind of labor, though

Reasons why some have larger shares than others.

put forth by fewer individuals, than to physical exertion. There is, however, no doubt that this fact is taken advantage of in different ways by employers, and that the laborers for wages, as we may see later, are often the victims of gross injustice.

The right of property, then, must be held to be a natural right in so far as it is the product of one's own labor. This constitutes the first right of property.

SECTION 2. — PROPERTY ACQUIRED OTHERWISE THAN BY LABOR.

A second right is constituted by **exchange.** If I actually own any kind of property, I may do what I choose with it provided I do not injure any other person. If *Philosophy of* I have made more shoes than I need for my own *exchange.* use, and if one of my neighbors has produced more wheat than he can consume, and if another neighbor has caught more fish than he wants, and if both of these are in want of shoes and I have not a supply of the commodities which they have produced, I may exchange my surplus for their surplus, and thus each will be benefited, and each will own something which he did not produce, but for which he has produced an equivalent. Usually, very much the largest part of what a man owns he has acquired in this way.

Property may be acquired by **gift.** As the right of property implies the right to dispose of it at one's own pleasure, one may convey a portion or the whole of his property to another and thus surrender his right to him. In such a case, the right to the property inheres in the latter.

It may also be acquired by **Will.** When one has pro-

duced wealth, or in any way come into legitimate possession of it, most civilized nations hold that he may determine during his life who shall be the possessors of it after
his death.   There are, however, certain limitations to this
freedom of disposal.   If it shall have been proved that a
man was unduly influenced by persons likely to profit
by the disposition made of the property, the will would
most likely be set aside.   Also a man may not generally
Restrictions   will away property so that his widow shall not
of the power   receive a certain legal proportion of it, since the
of bequest.   law supposes that the wife is joint owner with
the husband to the property accumulated.   So, too, a
man may not bequeath his property to strangers, or to
benevolent or other institutions, to the extent that his
dependent children shall be left without adequate support.
But in general the principle holds that a man may bestow
his property by will, and the person on whom it is be-
stowed become its rightful owner.

Property is acquired by **inheritance**.   When a man having
property dies without having made a will, the presumption
is that had he done so, it would have been divided in
some way among his children, or nearest of kin.   Therefore, in this country at least, such a division of the
property takes place, and there is a legal order of relationship observed in the distribution.   It is not exactly so in
all nations.   In Great Britain and some other European
countries there are rights of entail and primogeniture by
which the eldest son, or the eldest male member in any
collateral branch of the family, holds the landed estate,
and keeps up the title if such there be.   This is doubtless designed to perpetuate the family name and importance, in order to which there must be property to support

it. But in our country, where the democratic feeling is hostile to anything like a privileged class or artificial rank, no such laws prevail, and great properties are usually, though not always, broken up when the proprietor dies. At all events, inheritance here proceeds upon moral lines, and where there is no will the government divides the property equally among equal heirs.

Finally the right of property is sometimes acquired by **possession.** If by any means a man is in possession of property, and there is no one who can show a superior claim to it, then the former is regarded as the rightful owner. But just here is a point of some delicacy. When I say that the present holder of the property must be regarded as the rightful owner, I simply mean that no other person who can prove no better claim has any right to the property. But this is not saying that the person in possession had a right to take possession or that he strictly has any right to hold it. He must be allowed to hold it only because there is no one who has a better right to it, and it is better that one man should be permitted to hold it in spite of the moral defect of his claim than that a dozen or score of equally defective claimants should be allowed to contend for it. The present occupant may have no moral right to it, though he has a legal right. No one else has either a moral or a legal right to it.

There may be a legal right while the moral right is wanting.

SECTION 3. — VIOLATIONS OF THE RIGHT OF PROPERTY, — THEFT AND ROBBERY.

There are many ways in which the right of property is violated. The first is by **Theft;** that is, by taking the property of another without the knowledge of the owner.

Of the more obvious forms of this there is little need to speak. A thief and his practice are both universally reprobated, even by thieves themselves. More men steal than advocate or defend stealing. But there are methods of taking the property of others, the immorality of which, though less obvious, is nevertheless generally admitted, but which the perpetrators would not like to have called by that name. Yet that is its proper and real designation.

A man may manage to get a ride on a railroad train without paying for it. He is defrauding the corporation, Different ways in which theft is committed. and taking for his own what belongs to others. It does not make any difference that it is a rich corporation. To appropriate its property is theft. Nor will it be of any moral avail to say that it will not be missed. Very likely not: still, it is a violation of right, and therefore forbidden by the moral law. This is given only as a specimen of a class of depredations on property which persons of no solid principles practise, and then excuse themselves on the flimsy pretexts mentioned.

Similar to these is purloining from governments. I do not speak now of the more obvious peculations of dishonest officials. But when a man evades the payment of his proportion of the taxes he compels others to pay more than their proportion, and this is equivalent to appropriating money that belongs to them. It does not mitigate the offence that it is a small amount, and that it is distributed among a great number of persons. The principle is the same. Moreover, if any considerable number do the same thing the amount becomes large and the unjust burden proportionally large. All waste of public or corporate property partakes of the same criminal character, and is doubly wrong. It is wrong to waste even our own ; to waste the property of others adds to the wrong by violating trust and adding fraud.

Embezzlement is another form of theft. By this is meant the using for our own purposes the property of others with which we are put in trust or of which we have charge. Of the direct and permanent appropriation of such property it is not necessary to speak, as being obviously in the category of theft. But men of not very lofty moral principles frequently make what they intend shall be only a temporary use of such property, expecting to be Temporary able to replace it before it shall be missed theft becoming perma- or needed by the owners. Clerks in stores, nent. cashiers in banks, treasurers and agents of corporations, trustees of funds, sometimes take money in their custody, and use it for speculative purposes, hoping to get immediate returns, and replace the amount before there is any possibility of discovery. Frequently, no doubt, this is the case, and no pecuniary injury results to any one. But the moral evil is none the less. Property belonging to another has been taken without his consent, and put to the risk of loss. More frequently the loss takes place ; and not only what has been wrongfully taken is lost, but perhaps much more, thus furnishing a temptation to repeat the crime, still hoping for a favorable turn. This may be repeated till the community is startled by rumors of a great defalcation, and the ruin of a reputation heretofore unblemished, and consequent arrest, condemnation, and imprisonment. Of the same nature, only as regarded by the public a more serious crime, is that of **Forgery.** A man signs his neighbor's name to a check, or note, or other document calling for the payment of money, and thus the perpetrator secures what is not his own, and some one has to lose it.

Another form of violating the right of property is Robbery, taking what belongs to another by force. There Property wrested from its owner by force. are many forms of this. Nearly always it is the stronger overcoming the weaker. There is not now so much as formerly of physical violence and personal assault for this purpose. Highway robbery was at one period very common in England. But with the advance in civilization, and the perfecting of the judiciary and constabulary, it is now very rare. There is robbery still, but it is carried on in subtler and more evasive ways. It is still the strong overcoming the weak. Carried on in recent times in subtler ways, but not less criminal. It is sometimes the strength which wealth or position gives. Advantage is taken of those who are feeble or ignorant to wrest their property from them. A man may be so situated, and his wants may be such, that he prefers to pay double the value of an article rather than go without it; or to part with some product, or give his labor for half its worth, rather than not dispose of it in exchange; and there are those who are glad to avail themselves of his distress, and become so much richer at his expense. Sometimes the laborer is compelled to receive the value of his wages from the store of his employer, and it may be to pay exorbitant prices. Sometimes a just claim for wages or commodities is made upon an unjust man. It may be a case where, if it were to be decided in the courts, the claimant would be promptly sustained. But he has little means to prosecute, and the other has the ability to make it more costly for him to do so than to lose what is due. Hence, rather than lose the whole, and perhaps something more, he relinquishes a part. The man who retains this is a *robber*, by whatever euphemistic name he may be called. So also is the man who takes advantage of the necessities of another, and actually compels him to sell his property for something less than its proper value, even though his robbery be carried on under the forms of law.

What is true of individuals is equally true of nations. When a strong nation goes to war with a weak one on some mere pretext, and then, as the result of National conquest, and the price of peace, forces the robbery. latter to surrender a part of its territory, this, too, is robbery on a large scale. Unhappily, this is not an infrequent incident in the history of the world. Sometimes there is not even a pretext: the war is carried on avowedly as a war of conquest. But in modern times this is rarely the case, and there is usually some more or less flimsy excuse. Some such have occurred in our own times, and even our own nation can hardly show clean hands in this respect.

SECTION 4. — VIOLATION OF THE RIGHTS OF PROPERTY, — FRAUD IN EXCHANGE.

The third method by which the right of property is violated is by **Fraud in Exchange.** I have already used the word Fraud in its general sense, but it has a Dishonest particular meaning in relation to trade or com- commerce. merce. As has been explained, property often comes to men by exchange. If we think of it, nearly all that men possess comes in that way. When we take an inventory of our goods, we shall find that only a surprisingly small fraction is of our own individual production. Men are so constituted that each individual can do but few things to advantage. His production is generally, then, of very few commodities; but of these he may produce many times the quantity that he needs, perhaps enough to supply the wants of a thousand others; but he also has a thousand wants of his own which he cannot supply. Hence, Exchange or Commerce, the surplus of each going to supply the wants of others than those of the actual producers. Here is an opportunity for dishonest dealing if one desires, as some do, to receive larger value than he gives. The moral law governing the right of property in exchange is **value for value.** An attempt to get a larger value for a small one, is what in common language is called *cheating.*

Law governing exchange of property.

The moral law governing exchange is violated when the seller gives in exchange a less quantity or a poorer quality of the commodity of which he is disposing than the buyer supposes he is receiving, or than both know he ought to receive. On the other hand, if the buyer contrives to secure from the seller a larger quantity or a better quality than the seller supposes he is giving, or that both know that he ought to give, there is an equal violation. The same law holds good for both buyer and seller, and in barter each party sustains both characters.

Methods of violation.

It is no way different in the case of the professional trader or merchant. It is his business to supply the community with such commodities within the limits of his particular sphere of business as they may need. His compensation consists in what he receives for his goods over and above what he pays for them. It is right that he should have a profit, and it is a convenient method of paying him for his time and labor.

Business and duty of the trader.

There is a temptation to make this profit larger by charging exorbitant prices; but this is usually limited by competition, as if his customers find that his prices are unreasonable, they are likely to go to some other trader. His success depends on understanding the wants of the people, and in having the skill to meet them both in kind and quantity; on his ability to buy to the best advantage of his customers and of himself, and to select the best articles; on his attention to business; and generally on his moral character.

The moral law in the case requires him to furnish good articles and such as are what he represents them to be, and to sell them at fair prices. There is no hard and fast rule by which these prices can be fixed, as they must vary according to circumstances. He should at least allow himself a fair compensation for his services, and he should not demand more than such compensation requires. Should he buy when prices are high, and there should be an immediate fall in prices, he must be content to sell at lower prices than those obtaining when he purchased. It is a part of his skill in trade to so purchase that he can fairly make a profit. If for any reason he fails to do this, the loss is properly his. On the other hand, if he has bought at low prices and there is an immediate advance, he is entitled to the additional profit. The advantages in the long run will thus compensate the disadvantages.

It is not his business to urge his goods upon his customers, or to induce them to purchase what they are not otherwise inclined to purchase, though he may properly enough give advice if asked. He is not required to explain the character of his goods generally; but if he is selling an article which has been damaged he is not to conceal that defect; and if it be one that is not obvious it is his duty to point it out. These and other kindred obligations bind the seller.

The buyer, whether in trade with the merchant or elsewhere, has corresponding obligations. He may not
The Law bind- endeavor to cheapen the commodities below
ing upon the their proper value, nor pretend the discovery of
buyer as well
as upon the defects which do not exist, nor bring to bear
seller.   on the seller improper motives, such as intimating the loss of custom if prices are not diminished, or other such influences.

It is not an uncommon thing when a man has discovered a very considerable value in a piece of property, which extra value is unknown to the owner, for the discoverer to offer the owner something more than the ordinary selling price of the property, but much less than it would sell
Taking advan- for were the real value known. It may be a
tage of the piece of land on which a profitable mine has
seller.   been discovered, or a lot where a railroad station is about to be located, or near which a large factory is to be erected, or which is known to be wanted for some purpose which will make it very valuable; or it may be some other description of property which has suddenly advanced in value, the advance being nnknown to the owner. The buyer in such a case gets for a moderate amount what he knows he can sell for a great increase, and thus becomes the possessor of property which would
Such trading have otherwise belonged to another. There is
not justifiable. among a certain class of business-men a disposition to justify such transactions. But I am confident that in the ideal society no such trading will be sanctioned,

nor can it easily be made to square with the rule of doing to others as we would have them do to us.

Sometimes men interested in the purchase of certain kinds of property cause false rumors to be circulated; as that such property is to suffer a great decline owing to certain changes that have taken place or are to take place, and thus secure the property at a cost much below its value. This is especially the case in buying or selling stocks and commodities on speculation. A false rumor may diminish the price of certain bonds, or shares of corporations, or government securities, or some material commodity, as wheat or corn or sugar. The buyer who is in the secret makes large purchases. Then when the false report is rectified he may sell at a large advance. Sometimes great fortunes are made in a day; but what is made by one is lost by another: the whole business is based on fraud. Corresponding fraud exists often on the part of the buyer as well as the seller. Rumors of a contrary character, but equally deceptive, are made to abstract money from certain pockets and to put in others.

Prices influenced by false rumors.

A different kind of dishonesty, though quite akin to those given, is practised when certain men combine to buy up all of a certain commodity that is in the market or that can be secured. If it is a kind of stock or commodity that is in great demand when the purchases are made by the combination, the price may be advanced to any point thought desirable, and the public may be compelled to pay the extortionat amount. This is what is called a " corner," a somewhat familiar term in late years.

Combination to control prices.

The whole business of **pure speculation** is of doubtful

morality.　By pure speculation I mean that traffic in
various kinds of property where no one is benefited un-
Doubtful
moral charac-
ter of all pure
speculation. less some other is injured, or where the gain to
any one implies loss to some one else; where there
is no increase of wealth, since nothing is produced.　In very much of this speculation there is not even
anything really bought or sold.　If all the professed sales
of wheat sometimes made in the Chicago exchange in a
single day were real instead of fictitious, there would not
be enough in all that region to meet the conditions.　A
transaction of this sort is simply " betting " that the price
will be so much at a certain time.　If it is more than that
when the time comes the seller loses and the buyer gains.
If it is less, the buyer losses and the seller gains; and the
settlement is made, not by a transfer of the commodity,
but by paying the difference between the real price and
that at which the fictitious sale was made.　It is gambling
on a great scale.　It is not only morally reprehensible in
itself, but it furnishes a broad field and powerful temptations for subsidiary fraud and false dealing.

SECTION 5. — VIOLATION OF THE RIGHTS OF PROPERTY
— WHERE THE EQUIVALENT IS IMMATERIAL.

So far we have been considering *material* and *tangible*
goods in exchange.　We have further to take notice of
such as are *immaterial* and *intangible*.　Chief among these
is labor of all kinds.　This is a commodity that must have
an immediate sale, as unless sold as soon as ready for the
Labor as a
commodity
and in ex-
change. market it is thenceforth unsalable.　To-day's
power of labor must be used to-day: it will not
keep till to-morrow.　There will be ability of
the same kind to-morrow belonging to the same individual;
but it will be to-morrow's ability and not to-day's.

In speaking of labor as an article of exchange, reference is had not to that labor which is expended by the individual producer carrying on business by himself and offering his wares in the market, as the small farmer, the village shoemaker, the cabinet-maker, and various other manufacturers, more numerous formerly than now, who sell their labor only in the form of commodities and not directly to employers. When we speak of a laborer, we generally mean those who work for daily, weekly, or monthly wages, and put forth their productive The wages of energies, not on materials and with machinery of labor. their own, but who go on farms and into shops and factories under employers either individual or corporate, and who receive the compensation for their labor, not in the articles they have produced, but in a supposed equivalent in money or otherwise.

The duty of the employer in all such cases is, first to pay a just compensation for the labor performed. It may not always be easy, amid the complicated conditions of modern production, to determine what is a just compensation. Unquestionably every man, whatever his labor, should receive the equivalent of the product of which he is the efficient cause. But the difficulty is just as great as before. The product must be divided between the owners of the plant and machinery, the purchasers of material, the government, the insurance companies, the compen- Difficulties of sation for the management of the business, just distribu- whether by the proprietor or an agent, wages, tion. and the legitimate profits of the business. With the exception of wages and profits the proper distribution is not very difficult to estimate. Perhaps there is no proper rate of profits. For the term as here used is narrower in

its meaning than that usually attributed to it. It signifies
little more than the compensation for the risk incurred.
As risk is largely a matter of chance, and as no man can
be quite certain whether his business will succeed, or to
what extent it will do so, the rate of profits which one
Risk and   demands is only measured by the amount of
profits.   risk which he supposes himself to have assumed.
A large proportion of such enterprises are entire failures;
a great number of others are only moderately prosperous,
while a few make immense profits. Apparently in many
cases, then, the wages paid will depend upon the amount
determined to profits; that is, if much is reserved for
profits only a small amount can go to wages. But this is
more apparent than real. For oftener than otherwise,
where profits are large wages are also large, so that some
of our ablest economists have declared that the two have
no proper relation to each other, or, at least, that they are
not in the inverse ratio of one another. The only means
at present of determining what is fair compensation for
labor are custom and competition, and it must vary according to the capability of individual workmen. There are
instances where obviously the compensation is not fair and
just, and where the employer is evidently securing the
labor of his employee at a rate which is unjust. This is a
clear violation of the moral law.

A second violation is when the laborer is not paid at
reasonable intervals, and promptly at the time designated.
Other viola-   Thirdly, when he is compelled to take his pay in
tions of the   commodities upon which the employer puts his
laborer's
rights.   own price, instead of in money. Fourthly, when
he is compelled to work more hours than are stipulated, or than
constitute a customary day's work. Fifthly, when he is

not furnished with reasonable facilities in the way of machinery and tools. Sixthly, when the workmen are compelled to work in ill-ventilated rooms, or under unhealthy conditions, or where they are exposed to unnecessary danger from the character of the building or the machinery.

There are other ways in which the laborer may be defrauded, but they are so similar to these as not to require specific designation. In general, when the **Advantage taken of the necessities of the laborer.** situation of the workman is such that he must take such wages as he can get or suffer for the necessaries of life, and the employer takes advantage of this situation to diminish his wages or to subject him to unwholesome or dangerous conditions, then the employer is guilty of fraud; and though the civil law may not apply to his case, yet he is morally culpable.

On the other hand, the laborer is under certain moral obligations to his employer. First, he must exact no more than fair wages, even when he has the advantage on his side. Secondly, he must perform the work **Obligations on the part of the laborer.** he has stipulated to do. This implies that there be no idling or loitering, such as would diminish the value of his labor. Thirdly, it must be faithful and honest work, no slighting or negligence so that the articles made or the general product shall be in any way defective. Fourthly, there should be no waste of material, or needless destruction of tools or machinery. Fifthly, the full time customary for a day's work should be put in, unless there is a stipulation otherwise.

SECTION 6. — STRIKES AND OTHER COMBINATIONS.

A question sometimes arises as to the moral character of combinations among employees, or what are commonly Ethical princi- called "strikes" to compel the employers to ple pertain- advance wages or to grant some other advaning to strikes. tages of which the workmen consider themselves unjustly deprived. It would seem that there can be no reasonable doubt about the right of laborers to combine, whenever by such combination there is a probability that they can obtain rights which they would not otherwise secure. No man can rightly be compelled to work when the compensation seems to him insufficient or unjust. It would effect nothing for a single individual or for a few to refuse to work. Their places might be easily filled, and they themselves would be left much worse off than to work at the unjust wages. But if a sufficient number should agree to quit work until their demands are complied with, it might induce the employers to grant their request.

There are, however, several things to be taken into account when we undertake to justify such a combination. Considerations 1. There should be a pretty strong assurance to be taken in the minds of the laborers that their demand is into account. a just one. 2. There should be a large likelihood of success. Even though the cause be a just one, it might not be wise nor right for the laborers to run great risk of defeat, thus depriving themselves of their wages not only while the strike lasts, but also possibly for some time to follow. This would imply for a considerable proportion of those affected much suffering. 3. There should be no compulsion exercised upon those who do not wish to join in the combination, no, any abuse or maltreatment of those who come to take the places of the strikers. To do this is to interfere with personal liberty, and it would be inconsistent to violate one right in the attempt to secure another. It is no doubt a great provocation when working-men are uniting to secure what they regard as justice both to themselves and their fellow workers, to have their efforts thwarted by the refusal of some to join with them, and that the latter should even so act as to prevent the success of the whole scheme. The temptation to use compulsion, and even proceed to violent measures, is no doubt great. But, after all, each man has a right to himself, and unless this principle is preserved, the principle that " right is might " will soon prevail. It is, of course, implied that however just may be the demand, and however allowable the combination, any destruction of the property of the employers, or any attempt to do them injury, is unjustifiable. No righteous end may be secured by unrighteous means.

On the other hand, we must on the same principle justify the combinations of employers to promote their own interests and to regulate prices both of labor Employers' and of commodities. It is true they run much combinations. less risk than do the laborers, and there is great advantage on their side. They also are much more likely to make an unjust use of such advantage than the workmen of theirs. The opportunities are more numerous and the temptations greater. Whenever they avail themselves of such means to force wages below a reasonable rate, or to compel other conditions unfavorable and prejudicial to the workmen, their conduct is unquestionably to be condemned as unjust and fraudulent. Still, I do not see how on general principles we can deny the right of employers to form combinations to advance their own interests. If this be true, still more is it true that this right pertains to the laborers, as being in greater need of such a defence.

SECTION 7. — BORROWING AND LENDING.

We come now to the application of the moral law to the transfer of the right of property for a limited period. In modern society, and under our modern industrial and mercantile systems, a very large number of people are in the temporary possession of property which belongs to others. Hence arises the relation of **borrower and lender,** and as nearly synonymous with these that of **debtor and creditor,** and the obligations that grow out of these relations. We may for convenience' sake divide the subject into three parts: I. THE BORROWING OF MONEY. II. BUYING AND SELL-ING ON CREDIT. III. HIRING OTHER PROPERTY THAN MONEY FOR A LIMITED PERIOD.

I. In borrowing money there are two points to be considered, **the risk** and **the use.** The risk is of two kinds: Two points to one when the lender depends entirely on the be considered. honor and ability of the borrower; the other, when the latter gives legal security for the payment of the debt; as when getting a loan of five hundred dollars, I give the loaner a mortgage on my house or farm. It is evident that the risk is much less in the latter case than in the former. Even presuming the honesty of the borrower, he may become financially disabled, so that it would be difficult or perhaps impossible for him to pay.

Let us consider first the case of the borrower who gives no security. He is bound in the first place, however much he may need the money, not to borrow unless he believes in his ability to pay. To borrow without this probability is a pretty clear case of fraud. In the second place, he is bound to so use the money borrowed, and indeed any other property he may have, in such a way as not to render himself unable to pay the debt. Thirdly, he is bound to pay the creditor according to the agreement and at times indicated in the conditions of the loan. Also if there be other conditions, as of interest, of which I shall speak farther on, or of any other sort, they must be faithfully met.

Conditions binding the borrower.

The borrower who gives security is under obligations to represent the property offered for this purpose just as it is. It must be free from incumbrance and from exposure other than is specified. In the second place, he is bound to keep it in this condition, and not to treat it so that it will deteriorate in value. Furthermore, if there is a failure to pay the debt, and the property pledged passes into the hands of the creditor, but by reason of deterioration it is not sufficient to meet the obligation, it is the duty of the debtor, if possible, to make up the deficiency.

The question naturally arises just here whether a man who has failed to meet his obligations through inability or otherwise, is released from these obligations by taking advantage of the insolvency or bankrupt laws. Legally he may be, but morally he is not. The design of such laws is to give a man an opportunity to re-establish himself in business without the annoyance from creditors, who by continuously pressing him with demands, or levying executions upon his means, might prevent him from getting upon his feet again. Many a man who has been compelled to suspend payment has,

Whether a bankrupt is morally, even when not legally, bound to pay his creditors. Design of insolvency and bankrupt laws.

through the protection of these laws, been able to meet all his obligations; whereas, if he had been pushed every day by impatient creditors, his case would have become hopeless. Nevertheless, this does not relieve him from the moral obligation to pay every dollar of any previous debt he may have incurred. The same is true when one's creditors come together and agree to release him from all legal obligations by the payment of a certain percentage of the amount due. They cannot subsequently collect the remainder by law, but the debtor is none the less morally bound to pay the whole debt.

Another question about which there has been much discussion is whether the receiving of **interest for money loaned** is ethically justifiable. This is denied by certain writers. The denial is sometimes based on the prohibition of **usury** by the Mosaic code; usury then meaning precisely what we mean by interest now, namely, payment for the use of money. The term has become diverted from its original signification, and now means unlawful interest. In justification of the modern usage, it is said that this prohibition is no part of the moral law, but belongs to the civil code of the Hebrews.[1] Also it is noted that the industrial and business methods of modern society are totally different from those of the ancient Hebrews. With them business was not carried on by means of great capitals. Next to no capital at all was needed for industrial enterprises. The borrowing and lending of money was like the bor-

Moral character of demanding interest on money loaned.

Relations existing in Hebrew communities, but not in modern society.

[1] It is remarkable that the representatives of the nation upon whom this prohibition was laid have been for some centuries the great money-lenders and usurers of the world, many of them accumulating vast fortunes.

rowing and lending of tools and implements and other movable property among our rural population. In such a community one seldom thinks of charging a neighbor for the use of a horse for a short time, or of a cart or sled, or an axe or a spade. Each neighbor accommodates another, knowing that he may need a like favor at another time. Among the Hebrews it was regarded with the same aversion to demand payment for the use of money as it might be regarded in certain of our communities to require pay for the use of the articles mentioned.

But, in our times and society, more or less capital is necessary for the carrying on of any industrial undertaking; and unless the credit system should prevail, some of the capable business-men would fail of the opportunity to exercise their peculiar productive ability, and production would be incalculably more limited than now. Hence there is a combination between men who have business ability without capital, and those who have capital without business ability. It must be also remembered that what is loaned in nearly all cases, though nominally money, is really some other form of capital; and no one denies that when a house, or a farm, or a factory, or machinery is loaned for a considerable time, compensation should be paid for the use.

The ethical law applying to interest is somewhat as follows: The lender is under obligations to exact no more than a fair rate. This will vary according to circumstances. If capital is scarce, and therefore the sacrifice is greater on the part of the lender, it will naturally be higher than when it is abundant. Then, again, the risk is far greater in one case than in another; and where the risk is greater the rate of interest may properly be higher. But the

<small>The moral law applying to the payment of interest, (1), on the part of the lender.</small>

lender may not justly take advantage of the misfortunes or straits of the borrower to extort a higher rate than he would otherwise demand. Nor may he urge upon him a loan to be secured by mortgage or pledge of any sort, and then, if the borrower happen to be crippled at the time of payment, foreclose and get possession of his property at less than its value. Sometimes this is done to a scandalous extent, and money-lenders enrich themselves at the expense of their victims.

On the other hand, there are moral obligations binding upon the borrower in respect to interest. He should pay a fair rate. He should pay it punctually at the time stipulated in the contract. Sometimes such loans are the property of persons of moderate means, and the interest may constitute their main dependence for support, and to be kept out of it even for a time may be the cause of much distress. But in any case one is bound to comply with the obligations he has assumed. It is not often that the borrower has the lender at a disadvantage; but it is sometimes the case; and it would be wrong in such a case to demand a lower than reasonable rate of interest, or when payment is due to compel him to settle for less than the stipulated amount.

2. Obligations of the borrower.

II. **Buying on credit** is another form of borrowing. If I purchase a horse on the condition that I pay for it at some future time, the seller in effect loans the value of the horse for that time. It is so of all goods. The same general principles hold here as in the borrowing and lending of money. The buyer is under obligations not to take the property unless he sees a probability of paying according to agreement. Having received it, he is bound to make all reasonable

Moral principles to be applied in debt and credit.

effort to pay for it; and no mere convenience of his own, nor the fact that he needs the money for some other desirable purpose, nor that it will require more exertion and self-denial than he is willing to make, can excuse him.

The seller is bound not to urge the purchase upon the buyer, nor to persuade him to get so deeply in his debt as to give him an advantage, or a control of his property, as is sometimes done. When such an advantage is incidentally or unintentionally gained, it would not be morally honest, though the creditor were acting within Advantage legal limits, to use it to the damage of the taken by the debtor. Years ago it was not uncommon for a country merchant doing business with farmers in his vicinity, to trust them to an almost unlimited extent. Some of the more improvident of these would run up bills so large that the merchant would demand security in the form of mortgages on their farms; and in no long time he would come into possession of the farm, perhaps at a forced sale and a cost much less than its real value, and this, too, after having made considerable profits on goods sold to these customers. I do not say that in all these cases, or in most of them, there was an intention on the part of the creditors to bring about this result; but there is always a temptation of this kind, and when yielded to results in a positive wrong.

III. The third division of borrowing and lending comprises all the cases of **Rental of Property.** Most of the same general principles prevail here as in the divisions Sense in already considered: but there are peculiarities which in the temporary conveyance of property which here used. need to be treated separately. The term **Rent** is used here not in the strict economic sense of that term, that is, of compensation for the use of real estate, but in the looser sense of compensation for the use of any property which is loaned. The borrower in this case, as in that of interest, is bound to pay the owner a fair compensation, Duties of the and such as may be agreed upon between them. borrower. He is to pay this at the stipulated time. He is to return the article at the end of the stipulated time unless the loan be extended by the consent of the owner. He is to return it in as good a condition as he received it except the natural wear and tear by the use to which it has been put. There is also an obligation concerning this use. The property must not be used in a way not contemplated in the conditions of the loan. It would not be just to hire a house ostensibly for a dwelling-house, and then convert it into a stable or a carpenter's shop; or to hire a lightly built horse to go in a carriage, and then use him to plough in the field or to draw a heavy dray.

The **lender** is under obligations to furnish such an article as he represents and as the borrower supposes it to be. Duties of the He may demand no more than a fair price, and lender. he may not demand its return before the stipulated time. If the property come back in a damaged condition, the loss must be sustained by one or the other party as the damage has been incurred in the way of the understood use or otherwise. If I hire a cart for the season, and it breaks down under an ordinary load and without being exposed to any unusual strain, the damage must be sustained by the lender unless he had indicated the weakness, and made it a condition of the loan that particular care should be taken in this respect. But if I hire a cart which it is understood is good for a ton, and I put on it a ton and a half and the cart breaks down, then I am properly liable for the damage.

The borrower is entitled to any **unexpected advantage** found in the property hired when used for the purpose intended or indicated. If a vicious horse is hired for the season, and hired at a cheap rate because of his character, and the person hiring him by peculiar tact in managing him finds that he is twice as valuable as was supposed, the advantage is rightly his and not that of the owner. So if a man hire a piece of land the productive capacity of which is supposed to be fifteen bushels to the acre, and under his management it produces thirty bushels to the acre, this advantage is his and not that of the owner. But if, as Dr. Wayland points out, he discovers on the land a coal-mine, he has no more right to that than he has to cut off all the wood that may be growing on the land and sell it for fuel. He did not hire the land for this purpose, and the advantage is not his.

The borrower entitled to any unexpected advantage.

But not to use the property for any purpose not contemplated in the loan.

CHAPTER IV.

CHARACTER AND REPUTATION.

By **Character** is meant all that a man is : all the qualities that belong to him, — his faults and his virtues, his purposes and convictions, his tendencies and dispositions, his strength and his weakness. **Reputation** is what others think of us, — how we are regarded by the community in which we live or by the world at large. It will be seen that these may be widely different. A man may have a good Character and at the same time a bad Reputation; or he may have a bad Character and a good Reputation. But I do not think either of these is likely to be the case. For the most part the Character and Reputation of a person somewhat nearly coincide, though it is probable they seldom do exactly.

Difference between Character and Reputation.

SECTION 1. — CHARACTER.

We are to a certain extent responsible for the character of those over whom we have any influence. Parents especially are regarded as having much to do in shaping the character of their children; and teachers, though in a smaller degree, may affect their pupils. In the various relations of society every person has a certain power over others for either good or evil. Probably no man comes into even brief

Responsibility to some extent for the character of others.

communication with another, but that he affects him in some way so that he will never again be exactly the same man he was before.

The general rule at this point obviously is to do others as much good and as little harm as possible. This rule is violated when those who are under our influence, and whom we ought to help in the formation of a good character, are neglected by us. It is an exceedingly great fault when children and youth are allowed by those who have the charge of them to grow up without moral discipline and instruction. It is bad enough when their bodies are neglected and their minds untrained; but it is still worse when their moral natures run wild, and there are developed in them all sorts of lawlessness, self-indulgence and vice.

It is especially a violation of this obligation when **positive influence for evil** is exerted. For one to deliberately attempt to harm the character of another, and to make him worse than he otherwise would become, is execrable, — it is something akin to moral murder. Men sometimes persuade others to act viciously and wickedly for the sake of some advantage to the person exercising this pernicious influence, or for the purpose of personal self-gratification. Where a man for the sake of gain places temptation in the way of a man, as when alcoholic liquors are placed before a person whose appetites are already deranged and easily influenced, or where one endeavors to corrupt the mind of another in order that he may secure his co-operation in some iniquity, that is a wanton and infamous wrong. There are some in all our communities, and very many in some, who are the victims of such evil influences, and some of whom are hopelessly ruined. These are crimes against humanity such as are rarely equalled by other species of wrong-doing. To steal a man's property, to injure his health, or even to take his life, is not so great a wrong as to harm and degrade one's character.

SECTION 2. — REPUTATION.

A good **Reputation** is among the choicest treasures that we can possess. " A good name is rather to be chosen Value of one's than great riches, and loving favor rather than Reputation. silver and gold." It is with many all they have to depend upon for success in life. Hence for any one to carelessly detract from it is to do a great wrong, and to commit an injustice not easily atoned for.

There are three forms of injuring the reputation of others : namely, **Slander, Backbiting,** and **Rash Judgment.**

I. **Slander** consists in reporting and circulating state-ments of the faults of others of which they are not culpa-Slander de- ble. It combines falsehood and evil-speaking fined. or detraction. Of the vice of simple falsehood we shall speak later. But the effort to rob any person of a good name, and untruthfully to put in circulation reports detrimental to his reputation, and calculated to make him Execrable to be held in disrepute and dishonor, is, as has character of been intimated, not only unjust, but cruel and such conduct. wicked and cowardly. It is all the worse so since the maligned party has no redress till it is too late. The bad rumors have spread and gathered volume as they have gone, till sometimes an innocent person comes to be regarded with almost universal execration. It is no pal-liation of the injustice that the individual who starts the rumor pleads that he thought it was true. He had no right to give utterance to the statement unless he *knew* it to be true, and not even then except that there was some end to be served besides that of creating a sensation by idle and senseless gossip.

II. **Backbiting** consists in unnecessarily speaking evil of persons, even when the statements made may be substantially true. Some persons have a **Defined.** malicious delight, a kind of " ghoulish glee," in publishing the faults of their fellow-men. They enjoy it as buzzards enjoy carrion; and when they have heard of some scandal they regard it as a choice treasure, and have no rest till they have divulged it where it will create surprise and excitement.

I have spoken of this retailing of the faults of others as unnecessary. There are some who cloak their evil purpose under the pretext that they are jealous of the good morals of the community, and they hypocriti- **Hypocrisy of** cally profess to utter the facts in their posses- **this kind of** sion only that they may condemn them and **communica- tion.** bear witness against them. But the untruthfulness of this pretence is very palpable. It is not necessary that every fault of an individual should be paraded before the community and become a matter of public comment. There are few persons who do not sometimes give way to temptation or commit some ethical error. Is it wise, and for the interests of virtue and good morals, to publish every such lapse from rectitude, and to condemn and reprobate the unfortunate doer of the evil deed? Virtue would make but little progress in a community where such a usage was universal.

III. **Rash Judgments** are those which are uttered in condemnation of character on an insufficient basis of facts. There may have been some wrong act on the part of an Malicious gen- absent person. This is discussed freely but eralizations. one-sidedly, and the sweeping conclusion is made that this indicates a general bad character. Such reasoning is erroneous and often bitterly unjust. We do not like to have persons treat us in that way, and to reason from isolated instances of conduct to general consequences. Such judgment is unkind and uncharitable. Frequently it is the case that even the single act from which this disagreeable induction is made is exaggerated or misunderstood, or taken without the mitigating circumstances which belong to it, and which if presented would have changed its whole complexion. If all men were to exercise this harsh censorship on each other, and then proceed to draw unwarrantable inferences, the state of our communities would be utterly intolerable.

Much of this detraction is inspired by a malevolent Character and feeling which possibly conceals itself from even malice of the detractor. **Envy** is not only a malevolent Envy. affection, but one of the meanest that can exercise the human mind. In the struggle for superiority men often forget that the only superiority worth striving for is that of real, not comparative, excellence. If I aim at a high standard of scholarship, and have determined to surpass that to which some one else may attain, it avails me nothing that I am superior to my competitor simply because either by indolence or accident he may have failed at various points. Yet so strongly does this feeling fix itself in some minds, that they are not only glad when such failures take place, but with bitter enmity in their hearts underestimate the attainments of their rivals, and take pains to get their estimate accepted by others. Sometimes there is added to the low estimate the suggestion, or something more than the suggestion, of unfair and dishonest means. Thus there gathers a whole brood of vicious and malicious sentiments, not only harmful to the person accused, but dishonorable and baneful to the accuser.

But it is not merely by open and explicit statements that this evil is perpetrated. It is often by hints, suggestions, innuendoes, and even by silence, that the reputation of another is damaged. There are those who not daring openly to lie, or to actually say what they wish to have believed, put on a show of virtue, and intimate that they do not choose to tell all they know, or that they prefer not to speak evil of their neighbors, or that the case is bad enough as it is, or that we all of us do wrong sometimes. Or they may tacitly assent to all that is said, even to outrageous misrepresentations. All this is done perhaps when there is actually nothing that these persons know to the detriment of the persons in question; and yet they could not more effectually confirm the worst impressions concerning them. A bold statement, even in a case where there is some truth at the bottom of the rumors, would not be half so damaging.

SECTION 3. CASES IN WHICH FAULTS MAY BE JUSTLY EXPOSED.

It may be asked, Are there no circumstances under which we are to give utterance to our knowledge of others' misdoings? There is little doubt about this. There are occasions when to frankly state the truth is not only permissible, but actually obligatory, even when it would harm reputation. An extreme case is where a man in endeavoring to pass himself off for something better than he is, and by getting into the confidence of certain persons, is likely to do them serious injury. A man may wish to borrow a large sum of money of my neighbor, to lead him to invest his property in an enterprise which he is managing and which if unsuccessful would be the ruin of the investor. If I know that the man is a mere adventurer and a swindler, or an unsafe man of any sort, it is clearly my duty to expose this dishonorable person, however much I may damage his reputation by so doing. Between these extremes of making known to others who are likely to be deceived the bad character of a man, and that of dealing with a person's reputation in the way of idle gossip, and thus needlessly trifling with sacred interests, there are many grades of good and evil in our treatment of the reputation of our fellow-men. To what extent we may freely canvass their conduct, or what should be the limit of our silence on such a subject, no hard and fast rule can be laid down. It is impossible to draw a line which shall be the same in all cases. But probably very few are in the danger of erring on the side of too much charity, though no doubt that is sometimes the fact. The great majority are naturally inclined to take too much liberty with what ought to be regarded as the sacred right of our fellow-men.

When a man under pretence of good character may be likely to injure another.

CHAPTER V.

VERACITY.

Veracity and Truth are not the same, but they are inseparably related. Truth is a quality of propositions Difference be or statements; and a proposition or statement is tween Truth true when it agrees with the facts concerning and Veracity. which it is made. Veracity is a quality of Character: it belongs always to a person. A veracious man is one who habitually intends to speak the truth. But here a distinction is to be made. A man may intend to speak the truth, and yet through ignorance or error may state what is really false. This is no impeachment of his veracity; though it may be a serious fault, and will go so far to modify the general verdict in respect of his veracity if the mistake is made through carelessness in ascertaining his facts, or if he speaks at random what should have been asserted only after diligent investigation.

SECTION 1. — WHAT IS A LIE?

A lie is not merely a statement which does not literally agree with the facts — sometimes even that is not a lie; but it is a statement which is intended A lie defined. to convey a false impression, or to make others believe what is actually not true. I may state what is physically and literally true, and yet so state it that I induce my hearers to believe what is positively false. For instance, a boy tells the Principal of his school that he did not buy a certain explosive in the city, that he did not bring it home in his travelling-bag, and that it was not thrown from his room. All of this is literally true, but it is at the same time morally false. The boy got the article in the city, but asked the seller to *give* it to him, promising to make it all right subsequently. He did not bring it to the building, but persuaded another boy to bring it, the latter not knowing what it was. It was not brought in *his bag*, as the bag was a borrowed one. It was not thrown from his room, but carried from his room and laid down in the corridor.

Illustration.

On the other hand, statements not literally and physically true are sometimes not ethically false, for the reason that they are not designed to convey any false impression and do not do so, since those who hear and read them are aware of their character and intention. Such are fables in which inanimate things and animals are represented as talking; also parables, allegories, and many other professedly fictitious writings and oral narratives. Into this category come many facetious utterances and pleasantries, the wit and humor of which consist in their incongruity with reality, or in their absurdity. Yet all these devices need to be used with much caution lest they mislead, and have the effect of actual falsehood.

Fictions not always false-hoods.

SECTION 2. — VIOLATIONS OF THE LAW OF VERACITY.

Men are so constituted that they naturally tell the truth; and it is only when the mind has become perverted by some other immorality that one consents to falsify. Probably a lie is always subsidiary to some other sin. A person has done something to be ashamed of, or something of which he fears the consequences, before there is any temptation to utter a falsehood. It is frequently thus that one in attempting to deceive is entangled in a compli- cated web of falsehoods, one being necessary to explain another, till it becomes almost appalling to any but the inveterate liar. It is also the fact that we are so con- stituted that we naturally believe what is told us. It is to be presumed that men speak the truth unless there is some obvious reason to the contrary. Hence the execration in which lying is held by all persons, at least in the abstract. It is regarded as among the meanest of vices. Hence, too, to call a man a liar is so put upon him the most intolerable indignity, and one more likely to be resented than almost any other. It is an unnatural as well as a vile fault.

Lies usually subsidiary to some other immorality.

The law of veracity is violated first when one utters as truth **what he knows to be untrue.** I say utter *as truth ;* for, as indicated in the previous section, one may utter physically untrue statements which are nevertheless not falsehoods, as not conveying any false impressions.

Violations of veracity.

Secondly, he violates the law when he utters as true **what he does not know to be so.** It is not enough that he has some authority for what he says, or that there is some reason for believing it to be true. He may assert such a thing as a matter of opinion, but not as a matter of fact or knowledge.

So, also, in reporting matters of fact, we may not **exag- gerate or extenuate,** as sometimes persons are tempted to do, either for the sake of rhetorical effect or for some worse reason, as that of prejudice or partisanship. Omissions of certain features are occasionally made in a statement, which, if fairly presented, would change the whole aspect of the case. So, also, remarks may be thrown in, which, while not in themselves untrue, yet may have such a relation to other parts of the story as to produce a totally false impression. By such means, and others that are similar, an ingenious but uncandid speaker or writer, without expressing a literal untruth, may, nevertheless, mislead and deceive more effectually than if he were uttering an absolute falsehood. Here, too, as in the case of slander, silence may play a delusive and deceptive part, and be as perverting as the most explicit untruth. There are many times when for a person not to speak is to confirm the false utterance of others and to be accessory to the most outrageous deceptions.

Untruths may be conveyed without being uttered.

SECTION 3. — LIMITATIONS.

The question arises here, How far are we to go in order to prevent men from being deceived? This, it will be perceived, is not the same as how far we may cause deception? The answer to the latter is, We must not go at all in that direction. But must we always tell all the truth we know, when if we do not tell it harm may come to others? If a categorial answer must be given to such a question, I should unhesitatingly say No. There are cases where even though some evil might come to the inquirer from not knowing the truth, more would come to others from his knowing it. I am now supposing a case in which an individual may have put himself in a position to deservedly suffer from not knowing how to save himself, as a criminal trying

Some facts that an inquirer has no right to know.

to escape an officer. I may know that if he goes in a certain direction he will be intercepted. I decline to inform him of his danger, even if he asks me. It is not in the interest of justice for him to know, or at least to be informed by me. It is therefore right for me to be silent. There are a thousand other cases in which, if I were to impart the truth to persons asking it, they might in a way profit by it; but they have no right to know it, and I have a right to withhold it; that is, in withholding it there is no transgression of the law of veracity. Discretion as well as veracity is a virtue, and neither needs conflict with the other. Still there may be instances of great difficulty in deciding what ought to be done, but the intentionally and habitually truthful man is not likely to go far wrong.

There are many other ways besides those specified in which veracity suffers. All **affectations and false pretences**, or attempts to seem to others what one is not, are at variance with a truthful character. There is such a thing as what the Hebrew poet calls "truth in the inward parts;" a settled disposition to know what is genuine and actual, to act upon it, to live the truth, and to scorn all conduct that would mislead another or convey any false impression of ourselves. To be frank and transparent and ingenuous, while at the same time we are sensible and discreet and modest, this is to have a veracious character, and to be noble and worthy of honor.

Enough has been said, doubtless, to indicate the opinion of the writer that an intentional and essential falsehood is never justifiable. Still, lest any should take advantage of an insufficiently explicit statement, I wish to remove all doubt on that point. I can think of no instance in which it is right

to utter a lie. There are extreme cases where it is
claimed that an untruth deceiving no one but a criminal
and wicked person, and told to preserve a life or to prevent a crime, is innocent. But I know no warrant for it
in any reliable authority or in the nature of things. We
have no right to do evil that good may come. The
moment the slightest concession is made to such a doctrine it is as " when one letteth out water." There is no
sure and safe place to draw the line but at absolute prohibition. The most that can be said is that some sins are
not as bad as others. But sins are sins, and we may not
commit them for any purpose.

SECTION 4. — PROMISES AND CONTRACTS.

So far the discussion has had reference to veracity as
applying to utterances concerning the past and the present.

**Promise de-
fined, and
how far bind-
ing.** But it also has to do with the future. A promise is something personal; that is, it is an
engagement of a person to perform or not to
perform some act in the future. Veracity requires that it
be made in good faith, or that the person promising
intends to do exactly what he promises, and that having
promised, he will perform it. There must be no equivocation or deception in the promise. The person or persons
to whom the promise is made may misapprehend its import
or the extent of its meaning; but if the promiser has
intended to state his promise fairly, that is not his fault.
He must also perform what he has engaged to do, not in
some way that will possibly answer the verbal conditions
of the promise, but in the sense that he supposed the
promisee understood it. Thus, if I promise to give a man
my horse in payment of past service or even as a gratuity,

having the horse, a very good one, there present, and he not knowing that I have another horse, and naturally supposing that I mean to give him the one there present, and I afterwards give him another horse not half so valuable, I have broken my promise, and violated the law of veracity. If I have made a promise, and find subsequently that it will be inconvenient for me to perform it, or that it will involve more sacrifice on my part than I anticipated, that is no excuse for violating it. I must do as I agree, unless the other party release me from the engagement.

There are, however, exceptions to these general rules. If I have promised what it is impossible for me to perform, then, of course, I am not bound by my promise. If I did not or could not know of the Exceptions to the rule. impossibility, then I am not at fault. But if I knew or might have known, and through my negligence failed to know, then I am guilty of simple falsehood. Also in case the thing promised is unlawful or morally wrong, I am at liberty not to perform it. But if I knew this when the promise was made, I am guilty of an immoral act.

A promise is not binding when made to a third party. If I tell my neighbor that I will give my horse to another neighbor, but have not so informed that other neighbor, I may subsequently change my mind and do the latter no wrong. Still, if the promise be of the nature of a subscription made, promising to give to a certain person or cause on condition that others give, then the promise is binding.

A **Contract** is a peculiar kind of promise. It is an engagement entered into by two parties, each of whom promises to do a certain thing or certain things Contracts defined. on condition that the other does a certain thing or certain things. The same general principles hold here as in other promises. There must be no equivocation in making the promise; it must be fulfilled according to the terms of what each contractor had reason to suppose the other understood the contract to mean; it must be fulfilled with the exceptions before mentioned of impossibility, or illegality, or immorality, unless the other party fail to comply with the conditions involved in the contract. If I agree to convey to a man a piece of land on the condition that on or before a certain day he pays me a designated sum of money, and if the day passes and the money has not been paid, I am no longer bound by my promise, — the contract is void. Generally the failure of either party to comply with the conditions of the contract nullifies the obligation of the other party. There are, however, some apparent exceptions to this, as when one joins a society for certain purposes in which all the members are pledged to do certain things: the failure of one or a few of the number to keep their promises does not absolve the others.

CLASS III. — DUTIES IN RELATION TO CIVIL GOVERNMENT.

CHAPTER I.

SOCIETY AND GOVERNMENT.

MEN are so constituted that Society is essential to their highest well-being. No individual is complete in himself. Each lacks something that another or others must supply; and each can do something that others cannot do; and each has something that others do not have. We find this even in the most primitive humanity. As civilization advances, the need and the fact of Association increase, so that they are always great in proportion to the degree of civilization. This does not conflict with Individuality; on the contrary, Individuality is essential to Association, since men associate only as they differ, and in proportion as they differ is their association. It is this difference that constitutes the individuality; and it is because of this that men have need of one another. For one man to undertake to live by and to himself would be against nature, and would greatly diminish the volume of his life.

Society essential to the completeness of the individual.

Individuality a condition of effective association.

Since, then, the natural and necessary tendency of men is to Society, there must exist certain conditions in order to its highest welfare. These conditions are mainly artificial and conventional from the fact that in the different stages of development, and under different circumstances, their social needs are different. But there are certain fundamental conditions that are substantially the same in all societies. Among these are the surrender to Society of the individual right to protect life, liberty, and property. It would be impossible for each member of Society to exercise this right to his own advantage or to the advantage of the whole. The weak would everywhere be at the mercy of the strong, and generally subject to them. The defence of the individual Society takes upon itself, and where acting justly brings all its power to bear against those who would defraud or do violence to any member.

Fundamental and universal conditions.

In order to this there must be organization, rules of action, laws and penalties for their violation; and to these ends there must be action by the whole community, or by representatives appointed for this purpose. In other words, there must be **Government**; and Government is the agent of Society for carrying out its purposes.

Government and its relation to society.

There must be **Legislation**, or the making of laws for the protection of the life, property, and liberty of the citizens, and for the safety of Society itself; as also to promote the general welfare in such ways as may be deemed advisable. In most modern nations there is a fundamental law, or **Constitution**, which comprises the general principles on which the government is based, and which fixes the limits beyond which neither

Govermental Functions.
1. Legislation.

legislators nor any other officers may go in the performance of their duties, and which also prescribes what those
duties are. This instrument may be changed; but the
conditions of change are contained in it, and are of such
a character it is not often that a change takes place.

Legislation is performed by a body called the **Legislature,**
which comprises representatives of the people constituting the society, and is supposed to consist of men who,
while fairly representative of the various interests of
their several constituencies, are at the same time men of
more than the average intelligence and wisdom. They are
not at liberty in the performance of their functions to
enact any laws that conflict with the fundamental law;
and if they should do so these laws, when ascertained to be
thus in conflict, would be null and void.

Another branch of the government is that which tests
the constitutionality of the legislative enactments, explains
these, and applies them in particular instances.
This is the **Judiciary.** It investigates the action   2. Judicial.
of members of the society accused of violating the laws,
ascertains the facts as far as possible, decides whether the
accusations are true, and, if the laws have been violated,
adjudges the penalty.

There must also be an agency by which the laws made
and adjudicated may be carried into effect. This branch
of the government is called the **Executive.** In   3. Executive.
most nations it consists of a single person with
whatever number of subordinates may be necessary. The
Executive may be elected directly by the members of the
society, or by representative bodies clothed with the elective function; he may hold the office for a term of years
subject to a re-election, or be limited to a single term, or

elected for life, or the office may be hereditary, as in Great Britain and some other European monarchies. In most modern nations, however, where there are hereditary monarchies, they have been so modified by constitutional and legislative enactments that the monarch is little more than the nominal head of the government, while the real executive is some individual, who, though in form a servant of the monarch, is actually the ruler of the nation for the time being.

CHAPTER II.

THE RIGHTS OF SOCIETY.

AMONG the rights of Society, the foremost is that of **its own preservation.** The individual, it is true, is not ignored nor suppressed; indeed, in the most important sense his rights are superior to those of Society, since Society exists for the sake of the individual. But for this very cause the preservation of Society may be a paramount consideration. Nevertheless, the rights and authority of Society are not limitless. They must be confined to the objects for which Society is instituted. If powers outside of these limits are assumed they are usurped powers, and therefore unjust.

Society and its members.

Society may, as has just been intimated, **protect the lives, liberty, and property** of its members. Laws may be enacted for this purpose, and penalties for their violation fixed and applied. It may call upon its members to repel invasion, or to engage in war where this is the only alternative to the destruction of its independence, or the curtailment of its liberties.

Protection of individuals.

Society has also a right **to levy taxes.** To carry on the government requires the labor of men, and they must receive an equivalent therefor. Legislators, judges, and executive officers, who are acting for the preservation and defence of the rights of the peo-

Reasons for taxation.

ple and of their various interests, must have their share of
the product of which by their efforts is made possible.
There must also be penal institutions and properties
devoted to these purposes as well as to other functions of
the government. The expense involved in these must be
contributed by the members of the community according
to some rule approximating justice and equity. In ordering this levy, Society is bound to show no favoritism, to
except none from the proper share, and to burden no one
disproportionately.

It is also bound to collect no more than is required to
carry on effectually its business, to waste nothing by
extravagant outlay, either in the way of compensation, or
Governmental on buildings and other appliances that are
responsi- needlessly costly. No exact rule can be laid
bility. down in this respect. What would be nig-
gardly in one nation might be prodigal in another. It is
not to be presumed that any considerable nation should
limit its expenditures to the bare necessities of its
existence.

It is maintained by some that Society cannot go much
beyond this without improperly interfering with the liberty
of its members. But in most modern nations the sentiment
is nearly universal that there are other most important
duties devolving on Society in its organized capacity.
Among these are the following: —

It may provide for and establish a system of **general
education** to which all children in the community shall
have access. Those who deny this right do so on the
ground that it is a violation of national economic laws;
that it is like supplying everybody with food and raiment
and other necessaries of life; and that it is better, both to

the individual and for the state, that each should provide these conveniences for himself, and as well the education of his own children. But there is a wide difference here. Men feel the spur of want in the matter of food and raiment, but they do not feel the like in relation to education : so that while some effort is almost universally forthcoming to supply the former, the latter may be totally neglected. Here emerges a great peril to Society itself. That the great masses of its members should be ignorant, uncultivated, and incompetent to understand the ordinary duties of citizens as well as the common principles of government, would tend to the destruction of the social fabric, or, at least, make the people an easy prey to the few constituting a privileged class. This is of special consequence under a popular form of government.

General education a political rather than an economical necessity.

Society may go farther than this in the attempt to protect itself. It **may demand that the children** of its **members have this privilege,** and require parents to see that this is the case. It is sometimes said that this is an unwarrantable interference with the liberty of the individual and the rights of the family. That is one way of looking at the subject. But there is a point of view in which it is put in a new light. The children have relations to the state as well as to the family, and out of these relations arise legitimate demands of the state upon them. Moreover, the children have rights as well as the parents, and among these rights is that of an education; and if the parent is disposed to withhold that right, it is the duty of the state to require it to be granted. Sometimes, as in a few of our American

Society may not only provide for the education of children, but demand that they avail themselves of this provision.

States, a certain degree of education is made a condition of the exercise of the elective franchise. This seems to me an eminently proper condition, yet in most parts of our country it is unpopular.

Society may also properly interfere **to protect laborers** from the exaction of their employers, and from the consequences

May regulate the relation of laborers and employers. of the disadvantages which the former incur by reason of their situation. By some this is thought to be opposed to economic theory; but many modern nations refuse to take this view, and are legislating in this direction. Men and women are often compelled to work in badly ventilated rooms, or under conditions hostile to their health. Society may require employers to adopt such hygienic measures as will prevent the sacrifice of health or life. Employers may also be required to provide all reasonable precautions in the case of fire, or in relation to dangers from machinery, and from accident pertaining to their business.

Within the last fifty years there has been much legislation, not only on the points just mentioned, but in

Progress in this direction of late years. reference to the employment of married women and young children. Formerly little children of five to seven years of age were employed in shops and factories, and even in mines, many hours in the day, earning a mere pittance to contribute to the support of the family; and the mothers of large families, besides having the care of them, engaged in mills or other places of labor every day, and sometimes the whole of the day. Public opinion, after much agitation, came to the conclusion that such customs were not only extremely cruel to the wretched victims, but that the strength and vital power of society were being undermined in a perilous degree. In such a case it was not only merely the right, but the obvious duty, of the state to interfere to compel a cessation of these hideous evils. Great improvements have been made in this respect in Great Britain and in this country, but something still remains to be done by government regulation.

There are certain enterprises of great public importance, affecting all the members of Society, which can be assumed by government with greater efficiency and larger certainty of success than by private individuals. Some of these it has already been the custom for many nations to manage through the government. Such are the highways, the post-office, the lighthouse system, and some others. It is a question agitated in our times whether there are not other kinds of business which might be profitably taken in hand by the government. Cities have in a few instances assumed the management of gas-supplies and of electric lighting, and generally of furnishing water to the inhabitants. It is urged by some that this supervision and ownership may properly and rightfully be extended to telegraphic communication, railroads, and street railways. Indeed, there is a class of thinkers who insist that the government should assume direction of all industrial enterprises, and become the owner of all the capital and of all the land of the nation. But evidently the world is not yet ready for the full socialistic *régime*. It is probable that many of the evils which such a scheme is expected to cure must be removed before socialism under any aspect could be practicable. It is not reasonable to presume that the great moral ills of humanity can be removed by economic meas-

Practicability of the assumption by Society of certain productive enterprises.

The world not yet ready for Socialism.

ures.   Ethical disorders must be remedied by ethical
means.   Yet it is not unlikely, that, as the moral condition
of mankind improves, Society may more and more be
intrusted with some of these great enterprises that have
been mentioned and as well with some others.   But just
where the line of limitation should now be drawn it is
impossible to decide.

It is generally admitted that the state **may prohibit
gambling.**   If any argue this is something that should be
left to individual responsibility, it is to be said in reply,
Gambling to   that such a practice concerns not individuals
be prohibited. merely but the whole community, and that
those who practise this vice affect multitudes of others and
are thus productive of wide-spread mischief.   This kind
of legislation, it seems to me, might properly enough be
extended to certain speculations which, though carried on
under the forms of trade, are neither more nor less than
sheer gambling, in which one man gains only as another
loses.

Nor is there much doubt˙that **many of the combinations**
which are formed for the purpose of transferring property
from those to whom it legitimately belongs to those who
have no right to it should feel the restrictions and penalties
of wholesome laws.   Instances such as I have alluded to
Combinations   are found when a few men who can command
to produce   large amounts of money, so manipulate the
scarcity and
raise prices,   market as to get possession of most of the sup-
to be sup-   plies of a certain kind, and then put up the
pressed.   prices to exorbitant figures.   If the commodity
be of a kind upon which great numbers depend, possibly
one of the necessaries of life, the factitious price will
enable the combination to realize immense profits, perhaps

some of them to make great fortunes, and all taken out of the pockets of consumers, many of them poor people, to whom such extortion adds a great burden. This, by whatever respectable name it may be called, is neither more nor less than robbery on a gigantic scale. The legislation of a state may find some difficulty in reaching such cases effectually, but earnest efforts should be made to do away with these great systems of fraud.

Somewhat akin to this is the formation of "Trusts," which has recently been devised, and is now in extensive operation. It is conceivable that a trust may "Trusts,"— be formed with an honest and laudable purpose. their possi- A combination of all the enterprises engaged lent char- in the production of a certain commodity, if acter. properly managed, would result in diminishing its cost, and thus make the article cheaper for the consumer. But by its very nature such a combination furnishes an opportunity to arbitrarily fix prices at a high range, and thus not only put what has been saved from the cost of production in the pockets of the members, but to add to the original price, and thus fairly rob the buyers. Any legislation which would prohibit, or at least regulate, such combinations would be legitimate, and come within the legislative scope of society, provided it did not trench upon individual rights.

In the great agitation now for many years existing on the subject of the **prohibition of the liquor traffic,** there have been on the one side enthusiastic supporters of Suppression the measures involved, and on the other bitter of the liquor hostility to them. It is not strange that, among traffic. unprincipled and base men, whose hope of illicit gain is threatened, there should be fierce and unscrupulous opposition. But these, unhappily, are not the only opposers. There are some honorable and no doubt conscientious men, of conservative temper and timid disposition in matters of moral reform, who do not see their way clear to accept the convictions of the majority of good men. This opposition can hardly be based on the opinion that these measures are inconsistent with the national constitution, or with the genius of our institutions, since they have been repeatedly approved by our highest judicial authority.

The only argument against it is that they limit the liberty of certain individuals. This, as a matter of fact, is undoubtedly true. But in any form of government it is essential that certain individual rights be surrendered for the good of the whole. Take, for instance, taxation. No law, nor any set of laws, has ever been devised that can make the taxes perfectly equitable. A large part of the population pay more than their just proportion; hence their rights are violated. But there is no other alternative but to pay such taxes as are assessed, or cripple the government; and if this is done to any considerable extent, the individuals who refuse will suffer more than if they submitted to the unintentional, but inevitable, injustice.

So the fact that a few persons are moderately incommoded by prohibitory laws is a small matter in comparison with the poverty and disgrace, the incalculable wretchedness, the pauperism and crime, the ruin of bodies and souls of millions of individuals, which may be greatly diminished, and possibly done away, by these restrictive measures. It would seem that only the most sordid selfishness would complain of the violation of any right likely to be invaded under such conditions.

CHAPTER III.

DUTIES OF CITIZENS.

IF such be the rights and duties of Society acting through the agency of government, there must be corresponding duties on the part of the citizens. Citizens The first of these is obedience to the laws. This have duties as well as is essential to the stability and to the existence rights. of Society as an organization. It is only as each member abides by the agreement implied in the consti- Individual tution of Society that it can hold together. It obedience the only is no excuse for repudiation of this obligation guaranty that the individual disapproves of the law. It of order. is hardly presumable that in any community every member will regard every law in the same estimation as every other member. If, then, a law is to be disregarded because it does not coincide with the judgment of the individual, there would be an end of government, and anarchy would ensue. Human laws at the best will be imperfect, and will bear imperfectly upon the different members of the community. But in any fairly intelligent state of society the most imperfect system likely to be adopted would be incalculably better than none.

Nor is it an excuse that the laws are not only distasteful, but unjust and burdensome. By the very constitution of Society, as has been already shown, its members are expected to make some sacrifice; and the sacrifices that any member is called to make are seldom anything as great as the benefits he on the whole receives. But suppose a conflict of authority arises,— that is, if the law of the state conflicts with the supreme moral law, what is to be done? There are three ways open to the individual in such a situation. First, he may obey the human law, and violate his conscience; secondly, he may resist the law, and violently oppose its execution; thirdly, he may simply refuse to obey the law and quietly submit to the penalty. Where there is a clear and obvious conflict between the civil and moral law, the last appears to be the proper method of solution. The individual honors the law by accepting without resistance its penalty. He gives proof of honest and conscientious principle by the sacrifice he makes in its maintenance. He also testifies his allegiance to the government by abstaining from any violent opposition. If it be asked, What, then, is to hinder any man from setting the caprice of his individual conscience against the order of the government? the ready answer is, that the sacrifice is always great enough to deter any except the most genuinely conscientious from taking such a position. Sometimes it involves loss of property, long imprisonment, great suffering, or even death. These liabilities are not often incurred on mere caprice. Except under an exceedingly bad government, such cases of conscience coming in conflict with the laws are not likely to be enough to perceptibly affect the order of society.

Injustice of the law no excuse for violation.

The moral law paramount and of supreme authority. Civil law to be honored even in its breach.

Under a popular form of government it is the duty of all citizens to use **their influence for the enactment of good laws.**

To this end they must have intelligent men of correct views, and men of integrity, to represent them. There are two kinds of serious faults to which citizens are liable. One is that of indifference as to civil and political affairs. It is sometimes said, and oftener thought, that one vote will not make much difference, and that the government will go on fairly well whether we give personal attention to it or not. There is also sometimes the feeling that politics are corrupt, and that it is vexatious and disagreeable to mingle in them. For this reason every year thousands fail to express their minds at the polls. A majority of those are likely to be upright and respectable citizens, many of them among the most thoughtful in our communities.

Duty of citizens in the enactment and administration of the laws.

The evil of such negligence would be seen if we would attempt to estimate the effect if all or a majority of good citizens should do the same. The making and execution of the laws would be left to incompetent and unprincipled men under the direction of partisan demagogues. There would be a lack of needful and wholesome legislation, while harmful and demoralizing laws would be enacted; and the execution of such laws as might be valuable would be impeded and neglected, and corruption and peculation would be common. We see such effects as these even now in our great cities.

Great evil consequent upon the indifference of good men to public affairs.

The other evil to which allusion was made is that of intense and supreme partisanship, and individual and local selfishness to which men yield their political action. Important measures, which have to do with the vital and moral interests of society, are sacrificed to the success of a party, or because some

Evil of selfish partisanship and local exclusiveness.

project which affects individual gains, or the advantage of a city or section, comes in conflict with them. Utterly unfit men are supported for office, simply because they are supposed to represent a platform, though they are known to advocate measures which good men everywhere deprecate.

It is the duty of all citizens enjoying the electoral franchise to vote. They cannot evade their responsibility under any of the pretexts previously mentioned. It is their duty to vote for good and upright men and for good measures. It is not an objection that they vote with a political party. Such a party may be representative of important ideas, and, in the estimation of thoughtful citizens, furnish a government that would be for the honor and prosperity of the nation. But no man should so ally himself to any party as to lose his individuality or independence. If he desires to adhere to his party he should be active in all its preliminary work, and in such primary meetings, conventions, and caucuses as are influential in determining its policy and nominating its delegates and representatives. To leave this important work to a few, and those not the most substantial and upright of the party, and then to accept the result of their action as the platform and candidates to be supported, is a grievous evil, and one not to be tolerated.

Duty to vote, and to secure the nomination of good officers.

It is also the citizen's duty to aid in the execution of the laws. It is only where there are good laws, and where these are faithfully executed, that liberty is at its best. It is true that there are men appointed for this very purpose, and that the ordinary citizen may be relieved from this particular duty. But

Personal aid in the execution of the laws.

this does not exempt him from all responsibility. When citizens are indifferent to the administration of justice, and claim that it is not their affair whether the violations of law are punished or not, it is an unfortunate state of society, and may be expected to rapidly grow worse. It is for the interest as it is the duty of all good citizens, as far as it is practicable, to see that the lawless and disobedient are restrained. In cases of obvious misdemeanor, for the citizens to aid in concealing the crime through fear, or because it may involve some sacrifice, is unpatriotic, and does not lack much of being cowardly. It frequently implies a kind of participation in the offence. To "compound a felony" is itself a punishable act, and is so treated by modern governments. There is a prejudice against "informers;" and there are no doubt instances when pragmatical action on the part of individuals is to be condemned. But to apply such an epithet to a person whose aim is to preserve the good order of the community and to uphold the law, is much more dishonorable than any act to which that epithet is thus applied.

Of the duty **to honestly pay one's taxes,** some intimation has already been given. The amount of these must be determined by either the assessed party or others. It needs no argument to show that justice is more likely to be done by disinterested parties than by those who are interested. To avoid the *Duty in respect to taxation.* payment on any mere pretext, is to unjustly throw a part of the burden on others, and is thus dishonest. To make false returns of property, or to conceal it by any device, is equally unworthy and immoral.

It is the duty of the citizen not only to abstain from all unlawful acts, but in respect to the great number of acts which the Statutes do not explicitly touch, but of which many may be morally wrong, to avoid also the latter. A

Duty to be public-spirited, to promote peace, moral order, and good fellow-ship.

public-spirited and patriotic citizen will not attempt to see how much license he may allow himself and yet avoid the penalty of the law; but he will rather strive to avoid all evil example, and to do as much as possible to promote virtue and peace and good-fellowship among the members of the community, and for these ends will restrain himself from conduct which can be construed into any sanction of immoral principle, or tend to encourage harmful action in others.

DIVISION II. — DUTIES OF BENEFICENCE.

CHAPTER I.

THE GENERAL NATURE OF THESE DUTIES.

As already explained, the duties of Beneficence differ from those of Justice, in the fact that the latter are those which our fellow-men have a right to demand of us ; while they have no right to demand the former, though it is our duty to render them. If a man has done me a service he may justly require that I return him an equivalent. But if he be hungry, though he have done me no service, while he cannot on the score of reciprocity demand that I give him food, it may nevertheless be my duty to do so.

The general obligation to do good to our fellow-men whenever we have an opportunity, is deeply imbedded in our constitution. The law of humanity in a The general greater or less degree is well-nigh universal, obligation. though often overborne and concealed by self-interest tending to selfishness. We see it manifesting itself in a community when an individual, even if he be a stranger, is in misfortune or peril by reason of accident. Let a neighbor's house be on fire in a country region, and the whole population for miles around perhaps will rush to the rescue. Let a man be reported as lost, or a child missing, and hundreds who have never before indicated any special interest in the individual concerned will almost spontaneously go out by night or day to aid in the rescue. Travellers have said that in every nation, even among barbarous peoples, let a man be disabled, or sick, or famishing, there will be some who, though they have never seen him before, and though he be a foreigner, will have compassion on him, and do what they can to relieve his wants.

It is true these are impulses of generosity and sympathy, and that they only manifest themselves occasionally. Yet

What such impulses indicate.

they indicate something in our constitution which prompts us to be kind to our fellow-men. But these spontaneous and occasional impulses do not constitute the whole of the duty of Beneficence. The moral law demands that **a constant kindness** be exercised towards our fellow-men generally, a disposition to do good as we have opportunity ; and opportunity of some sort is seldom wanting. Every day, almost every hour, to one who associates much with his kind, furnishes occasion to make some other person happier, it may be only a little happier, at small expense and inconvenience to himself. How much the proper improvement of such occasions by a large number of persons adds to the sum of

An addition to, instead of subtraction from, one's happiness.

happiness no one can estimate. It would be worth while, even if it were a considerable subtraction from one's own enjoyment; but so far is this from the fact, that it adds much more than it subtracts. Indeed, many have found in their own experience the declaration true, that "it is more blessed to give than to receive."

Not many of us are called upon to devote ourselves wholly to the work of helping others. Nor are we obliged to devote all our substance, if we have any, to this purpose. It is the performance of offices by the way and incidentally that is required. We do not have to neglect any other duty or violate any other obligation in order to discharge this. If the disposition we have cultivated be a kindly one, and genuine benevolence be a characteristic of us, there will be no lack of opportunities and means by which we shall be the instruments of beneficence more than we have ever dreamed of.

CHAPTER II.

MANNERS.

AMONG the commoner, the least costly, but not the least important, duties of Beneficence are those comprised in good manners. They are sometimes spoken of as "minor morals." In the classic languages the same word is used for both morals and manners.

Good manners included in good morals.

There are certain conventional rules of politeness as observed in good society, and sometimes codified in books on etiquette, which are to be observed not merely for fashion's and custom's sake, but because for the most part they render intercourse pleasant and agreeable, and which observed make men and women in one another's company at ease. But these rules may be scrupulously observed where there is still an entire absence of that kindliness of which they are intended to be the outward expression. It is quite possible to find men and women in our communities whose outward manners are nearly perfect, who never do an awkward thing, and make no mistakes in their deportment, yet who, it is easy to see, are simply conventional, having the outward sign but not the inward grace. There is no *heart* in the conduct. The most polished and externally unexceptional behavior may be coincident with a false and treacherous disposition.

Politeness does not necessarily imply elegance, nor vice versa.

One may "smile and smile and be a villain still." Where there is real kindness and a genuine disposition to make others happy, there is both moral character and real politeness. It is not seldom that rudeness of speech and of outward demeanor consists with the most thorough and hearty desire for others' good.

> " Howe'er it be, it seems to me,
>   'Tis only noble to be good;
>   Kind hearts are more than coronets,
>   And simple faith than Norman blood."

CHAPTER III.

DUTIES TO THE UNFORTUNATE.

THERE is no community of human beings in which there are not some afflicted persons. In rural communi-
Individuals everywhere needing sympathy, if not relief.
ties and small towns in our own country, there are not likely to be many who are in great want; though there are always some even here to whom our kindest ministrations are due, those who are ill, or upon whom has come some calamity, and to whom sympathy manifested is very precious. Such sympathy and benevolence are to a great extent natural and spontaneous in such communities, and scarcely need to be urged as a duty. Still, there are some who have little interest in their fellow-men, and who stand selfishly and coldly apart. To them public sentiment would apply the term heartless and unfeeling. There are others, doubt-less, who from a certain shyness and awkwardness fail to show the kindness that they really feel. But the moral education of our people has been such that in almost any community of such a character that most of the members know one another, if there is a distressing or protracted illness, or a serious accident, or a flood, or fire, or a bereave-ment, or any other disaster, there will be offers of help, an inquiry if any service is needed, and frequently much self-denial undergone in the aid of the afflicted. This is the

result of the widespread moral culture which is a large element in our civilization, and without which the character of society would verge on barbarism.

But in our large cities we find another state of things. Here are vast numbers of human beings living in abject poverty such as it is almost impossible for those who are unacquainted with it to conceive of. In tenement houses, some of which are rickety old buildings ready to fall to pieces, there may be found in a space which would be accounted insufficient for one small family in moderate circumstances, a dozen families living in the midst of filth and squalor, and under other most revolting conditions. Sometimes a family of several members will occupy one room, not very spacious, almost bare of furniture, with only an occasional fire in the coldest weather, scantily clad and in rags, seldom having enough food on hand for a decent meal, and huddling together in the night on a heap of straw to keep warm. In many of these wretched substitutes for homes, it is not a very strange thing to find a father or mother helplessly ill, with no medical attendance and no means of procuring medicine. What is indescribably worse, in hundreds of instances one or both parents are frequently intoxicated.

The misery, the utter destitution, and the famishing condition of many of these families, are absolutely appalling. In some of them the father earns a few shillings a day on such days as he can get work, or the mother by sewing for the soulless ready-made clothing houses fourteen to sixteen hours a day, earns a meagre pittance which seems almost as nothing over against the unnumbered wants of those dependent on her.

In London it is said that there are thousands who even in

the most inclement season sleep out of doors, — men, and women, and little children. Some of them by odd jobs earn now and then a penny or a few pence, barely enough to keep them from starving, but not enough to give them decent covering or any shelter. So in many great cities, within short walks of palatial residences and splendid homes where wealth is lavished in luxurious appointments and magnificent shows, thousands are suffering for the very necessities of life, and many dying because these cannot be had.

Now, it is not altogether because men and women who have the means to relieve this vast mass of want and woe are selfish and penurious and indifferent. It is no doubt true that some are cruel and hard-hearted; but these constitute a small minority. The great majority have hearts of pity, and would gladly help in any case of destitution or distress which might be brought to their notice. But many are ignorant of the misery that is even very near them. Others know of it in the aggregate, at least, to a certain extent, but are not acquainted with particular instances. Most of these and still others know much of the condition of these miserable multitudes, yet know not how to reach it so as to be of any appreciable help.

Failure to conceive of the greatness of this misery.

Real beneficence cannot go about its work haphazard and indiscriminately. It must have system and order, and some principle of ministering aid. It would not be beneficence to distribute even hundreds of thousands of dollars among the wretched families; nor would it be wise for the rich, even if so disposed, to share their wealth with the poverty-stricken multitudes. Such aid would be but temporary,

Beneficence must be systematic, and not at random.

and another week or month would find the poverty just as great as ever. It is a sensible principle that some men adopt never to give money to the common beggar except in cases where the situation is obvious. In most instances it would not be a real benefit, but only an aggravation of the evil that one would seek to relieve. One may safely give a hungry man food, and carry sustenance to a starving family, or medicine to the sick. But even this charity must have its limits. So vast a number of wants must be relieved, if at all, through organized and systematic effort.

In all our cities there are scores of benevolent associations which give attention to this work, and through which much suffering is alleviated or prevented; and yet it seems to make scarcely any impression on the great mass of human misery. Our philanthropy must evidently have a broader scope than the relief of temporary want. Nor is it enough that provision be made by the state, or county, or city. We cannot forego these methods of relief doubtless; but doubtless also they do not, on the whole, diminish the amount of want and destitution. The very presence of relief will make many of the improvident and indolent depend upon it. Several methods have been suggested as an improvement of, or a substitute for, those now in operation. *Small impression made by the great benevolent associations.*

One of our most public-spirited citizens, a clergyman and a philanthropist, has recently proposed that this matter be taken up by the religious bodies, not as heretofore independently, but acting in combination, and so parcelling out the city into divisions that each church should have its own district, and should be *A plan suggested for wide co-operation.*

made as far as possible, and a vast deal would be possible in this way, responsible for all the really needy in its section.

But after all, and even should the most nearly perfect system be adopted, only a part of the misery could be reached. A wise philanthropic scheme would look after the **causes** of this wretchedness, and not merely seek to relieve individual instances. There are four principal causes of the bad condition of the classes we are now considering : —

Four princi- pal causes of the poverty in our great cities.

1. First, there is the **tendency of the country people to flock to the city.** Young men and women who are in fairly good condition at home have a craving for the excitement of the crowded town, and the hope of making a fortune, as now and then a country boy going to the city has done. So they come in great numbers, many of them having secured no situation beforehand, and enter into the struggle for work, dropping down from one anticipation to another, till they are willing to take anything that will give them bread. They become seedy and shabby in appearance, thus making their chances of securing a good position less and less likely, till they find themselves in a nearly hopeless condition.

2. The second cause of this desperate poverty in the city is **ignorance.** It will be found that among the degraded masses education is at a low ebb. It is true there are considerable exceptions; but the vast majority are grossly illiterate. It is also true that some ignorant men are wealthy and prosperous; so that it cannot truly be said that ignorance is either a sole cause of poverty or that it is an inevitable cause; but it is answerable for a very large proportion of the want and misery of which I have been speaking.

3. This gigantic evil is largely induced by **the bad habits of individuals.** Chief among these is the **drink-habit,** though there are closely connected with it other vices, as indolence, prodigality, and self-indulgence. It is sometimes urged by those who would charge the whole responsibility for this evil condition upon vicious social economic system, that the drink-habit, instead of being the cause of this misery, is the effect of it. It is undoubtedly true that there are instances in which discouragement and utter hopelessness have driven a previously sober man into this wretched indulgence, with the vain hope of drowning his sorrows. Still, after all possible allowance is made, there is scarcely a doubt that five-sixths of the destitution and want in our cities are traceable to this cause.

4. Finally, a considerable cause is found in a **social and industrial system** which furnishes employment fitfully and irregularly, and which allows, perhaps compels, such large numbers to live in enforced idleness, or puts them at the mercy of unscrupulous employers who get their labor for the merest pittance, in thousands of instances not enough to furnish more than the meagre necessities of life, and those under the hardest conditions. It is not my business here to inquire into the causes of such a social condition. But about the facts there is no doubt. There are thousands of men and women able and willing to produce so much of value that the equivalent will give them comfortable homes and a decent support, and whose work, and the results of work, are needed in our communities, but who have no opportunity to use their productive power.

Now, any scheme of beneficence that is to do anything more than transient good to the children of want and destitution, must take cognizance of all these causes, and must address itself to their diminution or removal.

It may be difficult to devise means to send back into the rural districts many who have exchanged them for city life, only to be disappointed and rendered miserable and hopeless. But such schemes have been suggested, Gen. Booth's which, in connection with other remedies, seem plan. feasible.[1] The drink demon and the agencies under its control must be exorcised and banished. In view of the formidable defences which this interest constructs, and the comparatively small progress made in the past, this appears to many to be a hopeless task. But from the fact that some progress has been made, and that public sentiment is slowly though steadily growing to appreciate the perils which are involved, we may hope for more and more mitigation of the evil and its final suppression.

The illiteracy which plays so considerable a part in producing and retaining the unfortunate conditions, it must be an united effort as a part of all philanthropic schemes to remove as rapidly as possible. Provisions for elementary education of all children should be large and accessible, and all children of proper age should be required to avail themselves of them. All private benevolent undertakings should also look to the cultivation of intelligence as a part of their means of relief and rescue.

As to the fourth of the chief causes of the evils spoken of, it may be hard to find a remedy. Of one thing I think Economic we may be sure: this evil will not cure itself. evils will not I do not believe there are any economic laws cure them- which, by their own operation, will rectify bad selves. economic conditions. Here, again, General Booth's plan

---

[1] See Gen. Booth's "Darkest England and the Way Out."

may prove effectual. This would provide homes and workshops and industries in the cities themselves for the poor who are willing to work : it would send from these crowds thus gathered in the cities, such as are adapted to the country, to industrial communities formed for the purpose, and in other ways provide productive labor for them.

Another thing which we may take for granted is that no scheme will be successful which does not recognize two conditions as essential, namely, that the aid **given must not be so much for support as for the means of earning it; and that a large infusion of the moral element** must characterize the remedy proposed. *Two conditions to be recognized.* So long as vice and immorality are ignored or tolerated, so long much of the beneficence will be wasted. It is not desirable, nor is it necessary, to use compulsory measures of moral reform ; but all such influences should be brought to bear as will persuade men to be temperate and honest and truthful.

To bring such a scheme into practical operation would involve the union of many of the benevolent enterprises and associations now existing separately. The cost would be great, but probably not so great as is the present expenditure under the earnest *Union of the several enterprises now in operation.* but largely futile effort made in behalf of the poor. The government, too, should find some way to co-operate. It would be incalculably preferable and more effective than the present system of out-doors and in-door relief. The whole plan of government aid, though greatly improved in recent years, yet inevitably tends to perpetuate the pauperism it seeks to mitigate, and to destroy the manhood and womanhood that, after all, is about all that is worth preserving.

There are important elements of genuine beneficence that may seem inconsistent with all these organized means of applying it. The most valuable feature, especially to the subject, in administering to the wants of the needy, is **the personal element.** What is done by proxy or through the machinery of associations, such as committees and paid agents, however indispensable in many cases, still lacks the most radical condition. The bestower of benefits who never comes in contact with the persons whom he seeks to aid, and with whose sorrow he sympathizes, fails to secure for himself that blessedness which is greater in giving than receiving. So the receiver gets less good when it comes not from the hand of the bestower with the kindly word and the assurance of something better than mere material good.

The personal element essential.

It is sometimes the case that men by a pecuniary commutation hope to purchase for themselves an exemption from personal contact with suffering and want which shock and annoy them. But such givers can seldom know the rewards of real beneficence. It is true that in great plans for removing the immense evils of which we speak there must be much machinery and many agents; but this should not, as it certainty need not, exclude personal beneficence.

CHAPTER IV.

BENEFICENCE TO THE CRIMINAL CLASSES.

A VERY large proportion of those to whom it is our duty to do good are not virtuous persons. But if a man has become vicious he is not therefore incapable of a return to righteous ways. The greatest kindness we can do him is to induce this return. It may be necessary to punish him, or in some way more or less painful to make him realize the unprofitableness of wrong-doing. Punishment But this alone will not always win the wicked. not a sufficient reform-We can do a person little good unless we can atory means. convince him that we have a kindly feeling towards him. It is often the case that when a young man has fallen into evil ways and begins to realize the disapprobation of public sentiment, he comes to feel that good people are hostile to him, and this very feeling drives him further into wrong-doing. If in such cases the truly benevolent can only evince their benevolence to such an one, and make him realize that there are charity and sympathy for him, he may be easily rescued.

It is one of the unfortunate conditions of a criminal who has been detected and passed a period of The social obstacles to the reformation of criminals. imprisonment, that on his release every one is distrustful of him. No one cares to employ him. He is an outcast, and it is nearly impossible for him to gain a footing in society. Such a person is almost driven again into crime. If persons when set free could be met at their prison doors by those who are really

Remedies. friendly, and who will care for them for a time, and see that they have work till their disposition to reform is tested, and then recommend them to employers who need their labor, thousands of such persons would be restored to manhood, and, instead of remaining outcasts, would become respectable citizens. But here, as everywhere else in our benevolent undertakings, we must not trust too much to the machinery of associations. Personal effort is the only effectual way of reaching individuals of this class.

CHAPTER V.

BENEFICENCE TO OUR ENEMIES.

A BENEVOLENT feeling towards those who are hostile to us is none the less a duty, because it involves some sacrifice on our part. The first spontaneous impulse The spirit of when one has injured us is to retaliate. If this retaliation to be sup- impulse were to control men universally, it is pressed. easy to see that the consequences would be most deplorable. When we are injured, and allow free scope to our resentment, the excitement we are under renders us quite unfit to judge between ourselves and the offending party. We are pretty sure to overestimate the amount of harm received. We are also incompetent to determine the amount of retaliatory harm we are inflicting. Add to this double miscalculation on our part, the double miscalculation our adversary is likely to make, and we see that in any individual instances the estimates are likely to differ widely, and both are greatly unjust. If I inflict upon him the evil that I think he deserves, there will in his judgment be a large balance due me which he may proceed to inflict. Evidently, in this way endless quarrels, criminations, and recriminations will go on ; and if this spirit is universal, society will become an arena of ill-will, bitter strife, and moral confusion which it is painful to contemplate.

On the other hand, to treat our enemies with kindness, to exercise patience and charity to those who have neither towards us, to accept without retaliation, and to give a soft answer to an ebullition of wrath, indicate a noble and generous spirit, and a power of self-control which is Moral effect of a generous kindness. among the most valuable attributes of a human soul. Nothing so much tends to bring an offender to a sense of his own wrong doing and wrong feeling, while it mightily promotes the peace and harmony of the community. The Christian religion enjoins the forgiveness of injuries, and the love of our enemies; and theoretically there are few who doubt the desirableness of such a disposition.

This does not imply that we are to treat crime as though it were of no consequence, or to stand between Compatible with strict justice. Society and the punishment of the violation of law. We may properly, and without any violation of the obligations of benevolence, aid in bringing evil-doers to justice; but this because we should love the whole community more than any individual. While we co-operate in the execution of the laws, even if the results should be imprisonment or death, we may do this with no evil animus, and may desire most heartily to benefit the transgressor to the whole extent of our power.

PART III.

DUTIES TO GOD.

211

DUTIES TO GOD.

CHAPTER I.

LOVE IN ITS RELATION TO THE MORAL LAW.

It has been shown by many writers that the whole range of duties to God and our fellow-men is comprehended in the one word Love. It is the very essence of love to inspire the subject of it with a desire to please the object loved. Hence, to love God with all the heart, is to desire above all things to please him, and to do what he desires us to do. So, also, if we love our fellow-men we will desire to render them happy, and to abstain from whatever is disagreeable to them. So our Scriptures say with remarkable truthfulness, "Love is the fulfilling of the law." It is unquestionable that the completeness of love in the human soul would lead that soul to comply with all moral requirements. *How Love fulfils the law.*

In such a soul it is evident that the feeling of obligation and duty would be virtually lost, and men would perform the acts which these terms imply, not because they are binding upon them, but because they want to do them. There would be no restraint nor constraint, but perfect obedience and yet perfect freedom. *Effect on the subject.*

213

Men would be perfectly adjusted to their conditions, and the laws of their being, and self-denial and sacrifice, and the disagreeableness of duty, would in a sense become Love not yet obsolete. But to this state most men have not so abounding yet attained; and the great mass of us still as to preclude the necessity feel the pressure of obligation, and right con- of sacrifice. duct will involve duties more or less burdensome and irksome. Hence, the impracticability of leaving our actions to spontaneous impulses, and the necessity of explicit precepts and formal rules of action.

CHAPTER II.

DUTIES GROWING OUT OF OUR IMMEDIATE RELATION TO GOD.

A BRIEF survey of our relations to God will prepare us to discern more readily and clearly the obligations we are under to him, and the nature of the duties we owe him.

There are certain characteristics which all who believe in a personal God attribute to him. He is regarded as our Creator, and the Creator of all the conditions and concomitants of our existence. He constantly upholds and provides for us, and without this support we should remedilessly perish. Hence, our relation to him is that of absolute dependence. "In him we live and move and have our being." By the very fact of creation he has entire proprietorship in us. He has a right to do whatever he sees best with us. We are under obligations to submit to him, and to do whatever he may require at our hands. *The Divine character, and our relations to the Divine Being.*

In the second place, he is a Being of all conceivable excellences, of power, wisdom, justice, goodness, love, purity, and holiness; and these are so harmonized and blended that they form a character of transcendent moral beauty. Furthermore, we are constituted to love and admire just these qualities above all others. Hence, in our moral condition we cannot be otherwise than irresistibly attracted by them if once we know them.

Again, God has been exercising the powers implied in these attributes for our good ever since we were born; and this not because of any obligation on his part, but freely, spontaneously, and graciously; so that there must naturally arise in an unperverted human soul, not merely a marvellous delight in contemplating such a character, but a feeling of the most profound and glowing gratitude.

Out of these relations, and the natural feelings that are excited by a contemplation of them, grow a variety of duties and obligations. Among the most definite and obvious of these are those of Worship, of Sabbath Observance, and of Studying the Holy Scriptures.

SECTION 1. — WORSHIP.

In all the diverse religions of the world, even in those most corrupt and preposterous, the idea of worship has been the most constant and the most prominent. Addresses and offerings to Deity are present in them all. In ancient times, the latter consisted largely in the form of sacrifices and material offerings. In the later development of the race, this tends more towards the spiritual, and embraces adoration, praise, thanksgiving, confession for sin, petition for forgiveness and for help in the temptations and trials of life. By this means man is brought into communion with his Maker, he is made to contemplate the Divine character, and thus to be changed into the same image. He also reflects upon his own wants, and is more ready to discern the provisions for these wants, and the remedies for his moral ailments. Men of undevout spirit and of a scepti-

Character and effect of worship.

cal disposition sometimes deny the efficacy of prayer, declaring that it changes nothing, and that it is unphilosophical to regard God as doing anything because men pray that he would not do if they do not pray. Yet all the causes and conditions on which all things in the universe depend, and all events turn, are appointed by God, and among them are hundreds for which we know no reason: the secret of them rests with the Creator. We do know that men sometimes furnish the conditions on which God produces certain effects. It is clearly within the range of possibilities that prayer may be a condition of this very kind. But in any case, it is obvious that the spirit of man thus brought into intercourse with the Infinite and Eternal Spirit, dwelling upon his perfections, and reflecting upon his requirements, and the obligations corresponding to them, cannot but be purified, elevated, enlarged, and ennobled.

Reasonableness and efficacy of prayer.

SECTION 2. — A SPECIAL DAY FOR RELIGIOUS OBSERVANCE.

That there should be some special time set apart for religious observance is neither unnatural nor unreasonable. It is true that our relations to God are such that all our time should be devoted to his service. But as in most other important matters we set apart special seasons to their more particular considerations, so here. Among Christians one day in seven is thus devoted to special religious exercise. It is an ancient ordinance, established early in the history of the race, and has been observed by a certain portion of it through all the generations. The value of such sequestration of time should be

The setting apart of a special day for religious observance.

obvious even to those who have no regard for the authority claimed for it. The physical and mental advantage of periodical seasons of rest and recuperation, recognized by eminent medical authorities, the benefit accruing to the spiritual nature, the increase of religious knowledge coming from instruction, reading, meditation, and the inspiration and courage gathered from such opportunities, cannot be estimated.

How the day should be spent so as to meet the ethical requirement involved, is worthy of some consideration. In the first place, it should be **a day of rest.** This does not mean that it should be a day of sloth and idleness. There would be no refreshment nor spiritual invigoration in such a day. Periods of vacuity and inanity usually add nothing to the value of one's existence except in cases of prostration and debilitation from overexertion. The rest to which such a season may be reasonably devoted is compatible with more or less activity of a kind wholly different from that of the secular days, and directed either to moral and spiritual self-culture or to some effort for the good of others. Genuine rest is found rather in a change of occupation than in cessation from exertion.

Idleness and indolence not always rest.

In the second place, it should be a part of the observance of the day to bring the mind to **a contemplation of moral and spiritual truth.** That men should devote a portion of the sacred day to assembling together, uniting their devotions, and listening to the word of instruction, appears rational and sensible. There are also opportunities afforded by such a day to aid in the religious training of the young, to visit and minister to the sick and unfortunate, to assist in mutual moral culture, as well as to engage in private reading and meditation. It certainly is not part of the requirements of such a day to make it, by a mistaken rigidity, disagreeable and offensive to the young, so that they will deprecate its coming, and Not to be rejoice when it is gone. There are many house- made disa-greeable and holds where it is a day of delights, of enjoyable offensive. exercise, and of happy experiences, better than all the other days of the week.

SECTION 3. — THE STUDY OF THE SCRIPTURES.

It is the belief of Christians, that in addition to the light of nature, God has given to us a more special revelation of his will and our duty in the form of **Holy Scriptures.** Here are accounts of the early moral history of the human race, of God's dealings with them, of the process of religious education of humanity, of the nature Contents of sin and holiness, of the character of God of the and of man's relation to him, of the means for Scriptures. our redemption, of the mission of Jesus Christ, the record of his wondrous character and works and the means used by him to effect that restoration, of the example he set of perfect human conduct, and the injunction he laid upon his followers to propagate his doctrines and methods of living, and of the efforts put forth by them in spreading his religion in the earth.

It contains in all parts of it moral and spiritual commandments, accompanied by penal sanctions, and by promises of rewards, grand object lessons of noble conduct on the part of individuals, and instances of moral heroism, offset by pictures of personal wickedness, appalling apostasy and condign punishments.

Such a revelation is surely entitled to our deepest and

most reverent consideration and most careful study; and we are bound by the strongest motives to accept its teach-

Our obliga-
tions in
relation to
such a
revelation.

ings, and shape our lives by its precepts. If the children of a family are under obligation to attend to the statements of a father in re- spect to conduct, and to submissively accept his instructions and apply them in their lives, how much more is it our duty to regard the Divine revelation as paramount, to study it constantly and diligently, and to make its counsels the guide of our lives.

CHAPTER III.

THE RELIGIOUS USE OF ALL OUR POWERS.

IT is not exclusively in special classes of duties such as have been named, that we are to discharge our obligations to God. By his very nature we owe him the whole service of our lives. Nor is this service such as to subtract from our own interests or advantage, as it might conceivably do and still be obligatory. He has graciously ordained, in accordance with his own disposition towards us, that every service demanded by him also redounds to our own welfare. Entire devotion to his interests results in the highest possible degree to the promotion of our own. *Not by the performance of special duties that we can discharge our religious obligations.*

Devotion, then, to the service of God does not by any means imply that we are to make our lives uninteresting or unenjoyable. Christian self-denial does not mean that we are to go out of our way to find disagreeable duties, simply because they are disagreeable. God has designed for us the very *Religious service does not imply the making of life unhappy.* highest conceivable happiness, and we are never called upon to sacrifice pleasure unless it is in conflict with some higher and nobler pleasure.

SECTION 1. — THE SERVICE OF OUR BODIES.

This devotion of all our powers to the Divine service implies first, that we serve God with our physical powers. There are right ways and wrong ways of using our bodies. That we should have bodies of the highest utility and greatest value to ourselves, perfectly coincides with our having bodies most effective for the Divine service. That Physical they are to be the instruments of our souls, and members to be strong, healthy, capable of endurance, and be as instruments of the not instruments of mere sensual gratification, soul, strong and healthy subject to lusts and passions, defiled, debilitated, and effective. and rendered incompetent by excess, is as clearly God's will as it is the dictate of broad and enlightened self-interest. Hence, to keep the body in condition for God's service, is equivalent to having it in condition for our own highest interest and enjoyment. This service The service here required is not something not abstract separate and abstract from common human from common human inter- interests. On the contrary, the Divine demands ests. on our physical powers are for much the greater part that they may be employed to our own personal advantage, and the advantage of those dependent on us.

God calls men to all sorts of secular labor; and this labor is to be performed, not merely because of its obvious benefit to the individual, but also because it is an appointment of God. Hence, there is no man so rich but that it is his duty to labor, and in some way to be a producer as well as a consumer. So, also, there is no man, however lowly his lot, however severe his toil, but he may feel that he is God's workman. Every effort he puts forth to secure sustenance for his family may be also a service in the

Divine interest, and will be rewarded by the great Employer.

SECTION 2. — THE SERVICE OF THE INTELLECT.

It is not the less possible to devote the intellect to God's service. As in the case of the body, it may be a part of this service to make the Intellect as powerful as possible. Hence, the long years of training to which children and youth are subjected, in all the effort to gain knowledge, to discipline the faculties, and to secure the control of the mental forces. It is true that persons may go through all this process with little recognition of God, and no purpose of devotion to him. But on the other hand, all this process may go on with religious devotion as the foremost element, and where this purpose is not the less effective because it is paramount. *The whole process of training and perfecting the Intellect may be included in religious devotion.*

We serve God with our Intellect when in our studies we recognize discovered truths as truths of God; for such they all are. All laws are his laws; all causes trace back to him; and the whole order of the universe is as he ordered it. So in the study of the sciences, men are investigating God's designs, and are continuously coming upon evidences of his wisdom. *What implied in intellectual service.*

If in a semi-barbarous age, when men's conception of the Universe was only a minute fraction of what it is now known to be, when the whole of it might have been regarded as contained within limits less than the orbit of our moon, if, with such knowledge of the universe, the heavens seemed to the men of that age to "declare the glory of God, and the firmament to show his handy work," how much more now, when its extent has been magnified

All scientific truths Divine truths.

to man's conception a million-fold, and our thoughts are lost in the infinitude of the material creation, should the Divine power, majesty, and wisdom impress the student. No wonder that an astronomer who had made marvellous discoveries in his scientific investigations exclaimed, " O God, I think thy thought after thee ! "

Many years ago I heard Professor Agassiz lecture in Boston to a large audience on some subject in Natural History. At one point he was setting forth in his simple but effectual manner the skilful adaptations in certain plants, and the wonderful contrivances that characterized them, when the audience, among whom there could have been very few of much scientific culture, broke into hearty responsive cheers, he turned to them and said quickly and with much emotion, " Applaud in your hearts the wonderful wisdom that devised these adaptations."

It is not only throughout the vast range of physical science that the devout intellect may recognize and acknowledge God, but as well in the metaphysical world, though the studies here are more difficult than in material nature. But while there are scores of unsettled questions here, there are hundreds of facts in Psychology, in Philosophy, and in other departments of immaterial nature, which startle men by the vivid impression they give us of the superhuman skill which is involved in their existence.

Immaterial and spiritual truths.

SECTION 3. — SERVICE OF THE SENSIBILITIES.

The Sensibilities comprise that part of our constitution through which all our enjoyment and all our sufferings come. As the name implies, they indicate rather states of mind and conditions of activity than activities and energies themselves. As we have already seen, they constitute Springs of action. Still they have a part allotted them in this supreme service.

It has already been observed that Love is the one comprehensive element in all right conduct towards God and our fellow-men ; and love is of the sensibilities. Love as duty It has been objected by some that love cannot and service. be a duty, since it is not proximate to the will ; that is, no one can by his own volition produce love. It is true that love is not the product of direct volition. Yet the fact that the Scriptures enjoin men to love, and the additional fact that men universally approve or condemn one another as they do or do not love certain objects, indicate a natural conviction that we are responsible for the direction our affections take.

The truth evidently is, that every man feels himself at fault when he loves an unworthy object and also when he does not love a worthy one. In other words, we ought to love some objects, and we ought not to love certain others ; and this implies on our part a certain control over our affections. This is not a direct, but an indirect control. If a child does not love its parents, or a brother has been estranged from his brothers, while they cannot by a simple volition command the glow of affection, they can at least consider the motives and reasons for the exercise of this affection, and so, sooner or later, come into the free exercise of it. It is thus that men who have no drawings towards God may come to love him. They contemplate the excellency of his character, the goodness of his providence, the tenderness of his dealing with their infirmities and disobedience, the wonderful exhibition of his love in

the provision made for their deliverance : and such contemplation is likely to kindle their affection for him.

What is true of the affections is true also of the other
sensibilities. The desires which in the earlier stages of
Harmony of our being run wild to self-indulgence, and thus
desires to
take the place antagonize one another and produce all sorts of
of conflict. unhappiness, can be so trained as to run parallel
with God's desires, and thus become parallel with each
other, and free themselves from mutual conflict and its
consequent unhappiness. It is true our desires are no
more than our affections under the direct control of the
will; but we know very well that by checking the gratification of the harmful desires, and steadily resisting them,
they lose their power and may finally be suppressed. We
know also, that by plying ourselves with proper motives
we may strengthen a feeble desire till it becomes vigorous
and perhaps dominant, and even an aversion may be trans-
formed into a healthful craving. Inordinate desires become
hurts, and thus issue in immoralities and vices. They are
to be avoided, or, if they become actual, are to be reduced
to their normal limits. Even the appetites can be controlled, and made to do service for God.

SECTION 4. — SERVICE OF THE WILL.

In an important sense all service is of **the Will.** It is
the executive power of the soul, and initiates all acts of
The executive the body and of the mind. It uses these other
power of the powers as instruments. It has also ways of
soul. coming into direct service. The mind is capable of developing a state of fixed obedience to the Divine
requirements. In every man's life a time comes when the
question arises, Shall I make my own enjoyments the

paramount object of my action, or shall I subordinate this to the supreme law of righteousness, the will of God? The decision may be postponed; there may The supreme be vacillation and devices to evade the issue; question. but it must sooner or later, in one way or another, be made. If the latter alternative is elected, and no one denies that this is the proper choice, henceforth it becomes a governing purpose in the life, and all the moral acts will harmonize themselves with it and all subsequent volitions will be subsidiary to it. It will become a fixed state of mind, a kind of perpetual volition to execute this purpose.

Much depends upon the strength of will as to its efficiency for service. Many wills are weak by nature : hence the service is fluctuating and ineffectual. Every obligation to devote the service of the will to God also implies the obligation to render it strong and efficient.

All the duties which a man owes to his will as set forth in a former chapter are incumbent here. We are, as a part of the service of the will to God, to cultivate All duties to Decision, Penitence, Independence, Courage, the Will duties to God in Fortitude, and Patience ; and to discourage and respect of the extirpate Pride, Self-conceit, Vanity, Ambi- Will. tion, and such other vices as pertain to an infirm and disordered will. Whatever tends to render our will unworthy of God should be destroyed, and whatever renders it noble and worthy should be cultivated and greatly encouraged.

www.ingramcontent.com/pod-product-compliance
Lightning Source LLC
Chambersburg PA
CBHW020101030726
47498CB00006B/1886